THE HIT . . .

The Penetrator watched the TV screen with casual indifference as the cameras followed the senatorial candidate, Andrew Carver Wells, into the crowd. The rotund black politician was slapping palms and bumping elbows with an Afro-coiffed Negro youth when, suddenly, a small hole appeared in Wells' forehead and the back of his head exploded, showering those behind him with flesh, bone, blood, and bits of gray matter.

The fatally wounded Wells tottered backward for a moment, then crumpled as his knees gave way and he fell down face first. The crowd disintegrated into a welter of isolated individuals, faces blank, eyes glazed, mouths opened to release their screams of incomprehension and fear.

The Penetrator didn't know Wells. He didn't, from what he'd heard of the speech, think he'd like Wells if he did know him. But the cold-blooded murder of a public figure transcended personality and politics. The assassination of a candidate going about his lawful business was something the Penetrator liked even less . . . and he was determined to do something about it. . . .

THE PENETRATOR SERIES:

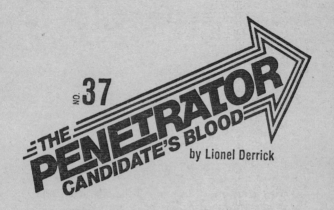

NO. 37 THE PENETRATOR

CANDIDATE'S BLOOD

by Lionel Derrick

PINNACLE BOOKS   LOS ANGELES

THE PENETRATOR #37: CANDIDATE'S BLOOD

Copyright © 1980 by Lionel Derrick

An original Pinnacle Books edition, published for the first time anywhere.

First printing, September 1980

ISBN: 0-523-40674-6

Special acknowledgment to Mark Roberts

Cover illustration by George Wilson

Printed in the United States of America

PINNACLE BOOKS, INC.
2029 Century Park East
Los Angeles, California 90067

To Bill Fieldhouse, *gifted writer, patriot and friend, who knows where the skeletons are buried in the real story behind this story.*

ld

CONTENTS

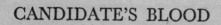

CANDIDATE'S BLOOD

PROLOGUE

Four men sat around a table in an Atlanta, Georgia, motel room, the heavy drapes pulled against the day's brightness, soft lights giving only minimal illumination. Their faces were grim and thoughtful as they listened to a report given by a fifth person, who leaned against the white-painted partition that led to the bathroom. When the speaker concluded his recitation, a portly, balding man in a wheelchair probed the blue-tinged, smoky air with the stub of his cigar.

"I still don't see what the hell we can gain by this."

"We gain everything, Porter." The reply came from a handsome man in his mid-forties, tinges of white hair at his temples adding an aura of maturity to his youthful actor's features. His sparkling, blue-gray eyes widened with candor and he flashed a broad, white smile of expensively capped teeth as he continued his explanation.

"First off, we haven't had anyone in the U.S. Senate to support our interests since your, ah, tragic accident. We need someone we can trust and this . . . ah, gentleman, isn't the one. We put him where he is for this purpose and he'll serve us well. Secondly,

1

what happens will be blamed on right-wing extremists, or the Ku Klux Klanners, or some such group. It will also provide a lever to pressure for gun control and eventual confiscation. All plus factors. And . . ." The speaker paused to apply a match to the tip of a pencil-slim cigar. He waved the stogy like a concert master's baton. "The end result is to leave only one candidate, to appeal to the liberal voters and the radical Left, who can also move into the vacant slot by wide public acclaim. Could we ask for more?"

Porter Carson rolled his wheelchair back half a pace, adjusting the lap robe that covered his withered legs as he replied, "You make it sound good. But there are still too many factors that can go wrong. It is absolutely vital that we have someone in that Senate seat who can suppress the evidence already collected regarding our mining activities and see to it that our continued operations go undetected. Millions of dollars are at stake."

"That's why one man's life is of no importance." The horse-faced man leaning against the wall emphasized his point by snapping erect and taking three paces toward the table. "For that matter, we can always arrange to cut out the guy who does the job, thus eliminating any connection to our group."

"You see, Porter," the handsome public-figure type soothed, "we've thought of everything. Trust me. There's literally nothing or no one who can prevent our scenario from playing out as we have designed it."

Despite the confidence radiated by those at the conference, they were not aware of, or had overlooked, one important fact. A man did exist who

2

could, if he knew of their intent, place a serious crimp in their plans. That man was the Penetrator.

Mark Hardin, known to nearly everyone as the Penetrator, was a large, powerfully built man of indeterminate age.

He might be twenty-eight or thirty-five, carrying his 205 pounds easily on a broad-shouldered, well-muscled frame. His hair was black, as were his eyebrows and the intelligently glittering orbs beneath them. His dark complexion—which tanned to a coppery brown when he had the time—hawk-bill nose, and high cheekbones attested to his half-Cheyenne ancestory. They contributed to his face, even in repose, a smouldering, critical look. When he frowned, a cold, deadly aura seemed to emanate from his inner being.

In motion, Mark had the litheness of a cougar, with the lean, hungry look of an athlete in top condition. He spoke little, using words only to convey important information or to inquire of matters that interested him. His accent, on those occasions when he used his voice, was CBS News neutral, but careful observers could detect a slight far West twang if they listened closely. Many times, though, the Penetrator's enemies never had the chance to notice . . . before they were dead.

The Penetrator sobriquet had been hung on Mark Hardin by the press. It had been while he was engaged in reducing Don Pietro Scarelli's Los Angeles Mafia family to a litter of bleeding bodies and smoking, ruined vehicles. Scarelli and his mobsters had died because Donna Morgan, Professor Haskins' lovely niece, had died in an attempt the mobsters had made on Mark's life. Since that time, the Penetrator had undertaken thirty-six other missions against the forces of evil that threatened the lives, peace, and fortunes of the little guy.

Operating from a secure base at the Stronghold— Willard Haskins' fantastic underground mansion built into an abandoned borax mine in the Calico Mountains of California's Mojave desert—Mark had taken on terrorists of several stripes, hoodlums, hate mongers, assassins, and mad men. He had even brought down an elitist, One-Worlder cabal that had infiltrated deep inside the U. S. government. Most recently he had acted to prevent a home-grown holocaust that would have exterminated the black race and, for the second time, protected the life of an American president.

The Penetrator's particular form of justice had been felt in ten foreign countries and nearly every state in the Union. He was not a merchant of death. Ofttimes he left the battered and bleeding—but living—bodies of his targets for the police and other agencies to deal with in terms of ultimate justice. Nor was he a dreamy-eyed idealist, confident in his own mind that he was leaving the world a better place for men to live in. A more appropriate comparison could be made between Mark and a surgeon.

When a cancer is found, the surgeon acts quickly to excise it, hoping to have gotten it all, but knowing that sickness is always with us and can strike more than once in the same place. Mark's rationale for being what he was, if he ever felt the need of one, could best be put in a way he had frequently verbalized it. He did what he did because it needed

4

doing. And he happened to be the best there was at doing it.

For the present, though, the Penetrator enjoyed a prolonged period of peace. The Situations Board in the Operations Room of the Stronghold was, for once, clear of any pending mission or situation that might develop into one. Barefoot, clad in cut-offs and a tank top, Mark Hardin had just returned from a five-mile conditioning run. He showered and started to dress for dinner, luxuriating in the calm generated by his freedom from tension and furious activity. Yet, he realized he lived in a period of false security. Mark knew that he could never be sure when or where mission number thirty-seven might begin.

Chapter 1
Death on the Left

All morning long a growing crowd had been filtering into Riverfront Park in Montgomery, Alabama. Their presence, in such great numbers, bothered Art Belman. The steadily increasing sea of laughing, smiling faces—black and white mingling without tension in a holiday atmosphere—presented a particular type of risk to Belman and his plans. A guy could never tell what a panicked crowd would do.

Art Belman carried that uncomfortable thought with him as he made certain once more that everything had been laid out in proper order. His route of exfiltration had been carefully planned. The narrow dirt road, at the southeastern end of which he now waited in a closed van, led to a residential neighborhood. Two blocks into the housing development, he would make the change to a second car, driving to the nearest on-ramp for I-65 North heading for Birmingham. From there, things would take care of themselves. No, that was the least of his worries.

The problems all centered around his present location and what would happen within the next twenty minutes. Belman didn't like the range—750 meters, only slightly under half a mile and over water at that. He opened the rear door of the van and sighted across the Alabama River to Riverfront

Park and the bunting-decorated platform a short way from the tendrils of thin blue smoke that marked the barbeque pit. Bending over the specially designed piece, mounted on a sturdy tripod for stability, he cursed as he saw a mil deviation waver up and down in the scope with each flick of his pulse. *Christ!* It was going to be some fine bit of shooting!

No sweat though. The bull-barreled rifle, chambered for 300 Winchester Magnum, and the nine power scope were up to it. It all depended on the shooter. Belman smiled, exposing uneven, yellowed, tobacco-stained teeth as he thought of this. Given all the other factors, he knew he could perform. In this business for fifteen years, he had perfected his skills with every tool of the trade, from such primitive weapons as a garrote or crossbow to the most sophisticated modern arms. He'd used most of them, too, at one time or another. His favorite, though, remained the OSS Spike, a four-sided, pointed, sharp wedge of steel that slid into flesh with a satisfying ease. He liked close-in work for the personal sense of accomplishment and . . . yeah, fulfillment that came from intimate, body-contact kills. They always made him horny.

Thinking of that, Art Belman felt a stirring in his loins and quickening of breath as his pulse rate increased enormously, his heart throbbing in his chest in time to the swelling of his maleness. *Oh, shit!* He now saw that the crosshairs of his scope varied more than two mils with each surge of blood toward his aching crotch. Belman reached out to close the van door. He'd have to masturbate to get his system back to normal. Otherwise he could never make the shot at this range. Sighing with contentment, he leaned back against the side wall of the vehicle, one hand fumbling at his fly.

Andy Wells perspired freely as he walked through the crowd, shaking hands, smiling, saying a few words to those who had been pointed out as hard-working campaign volunteers. *Only eleven-thirty and already hotter than the hubs of hell,* he thought with the usual triteness of a candidate's jargon. With one thick, black finger he tugged at the white, already-sodden collar that bound his neck.

What the hell—ruminations continued with a rush of irritation—*never could stand a stiff shirt and tie. Never wore a closed collar until this politics thing came up. Why did I have to listen to Johnny an' the boys tellin' me how I should file for the Senate? They fixin' to make me out a fool, what with him turnin' around to come out against me? 'Specially with him sayin' the same things I'm sayin! People at least want to think they got a choice.*

Damn this thing anyway, his thoughts went on as he slipped the button and jerked free the watered silk tie that was adorned with a "Dandy Andy for Senate" pin. He allowed himself to be steered toward the platform where a band loudly played.

Andy Wells took other directions as well, stopping long enough to heap a plate with barbecued pork ribs and one large, sauce-dripping pig's ear, black-eyed peas, collards, and a slice of watermelon. Then he was conducted to the gaily decorated stage. Every move, each gesture and word had been carefully choreographed by an agency man from the large Madison Avenue advertising firm that managed Andy's campaign.

9

He placed the double-thick paper plate on one metal folding chair, thinking how much he hated watermelon, collards, black-eyed peas, and pig's ears. He didn't think too much of barbeque in any form for that matter, but it was a part of his ethnic image, the ad man had insisted, something they considered most desirable. So he went along for the votes it might bring in. *At least, by God, those gray-flannel, trendy honkies from the agency let me say what I believe, even if they make sure each word has a proper semantic weighting according to their computer.* Sighing, Andy Wells got ready to go into his act.

Wells picked up one juicy rib and took a prodigious bite. Muching on it, he walked to the microphone. He licked his thick lips and raised one arm high, bearing the bitten-into rib like a choral director's pitch pipe. The music fell silent and those close to the platform turned their attention toward Andy. More people gathered and talk died out.

"Who-o-o-e-e-e! It's gettin' hot out here, friends. 'Cause of that, I ain't gonna keep you here too long. All I want to do is to remind you why we're here today. It's to eat soul food, drink beer, and have *fun!*" As laughter rose from the audience, Andy did a slow, well-rehearsed doubletake. "Oh yeah! An' also, by the way, to let you know I'm countin' on your vote to help me become the next junior senator from Alabama."

Cheers, laughter, and applause rose from around the platform, the band did a short chorus of "Happy Days Are Here Again," then died out as Andy bit into the rib and chewed rapidly to clear his mouth so he could speak further.

"Now, Brothers and Sisters, an' all my dear

friends out here, you know that the new election laws don't allow a candidate to say anything bad about his opponent, and in particular if that opponent is an incumbent in your own party. Well, I do believe in obeyin' the law. So, all I can say to you is that Nelson Lemmon's record over the past six years in the Senate is lousy . . . and I think that's good." Robust laughter rippled back through the trees.

"Why, he don't have the first idea of the importance of foreign relations. He voted *against* the Canal Treaty! He voted *against* normalization of relations with the People's Republic of China! He voted *against* SALT II! Now, how dumb can you get?" Light, scattered applause greeted Andy's rhetorical question. "What's worse, he doesn't have any grasp of priorities in domestic issues. Every year he voted for increased military appropriations. He backed nuclear power development. He joined the block that cut welfare spending. An' he threw in with the gun peddlers and the National Rip-Off Association to prevent federal action to control and eliminate the threat of firearms in our society.

"Why, everything the people were for, he was agin' and anything the people didn't want, he pushed down our throats. And I say that's bad . . . which means it's good. It's good because his record is what's going to elect me to fill the office of senator for this fine state of Alabama.

"My dear friends," Andy Wells went on in a lower, more confidential tone, following the cheering of the audience. "There are only a few things that are of real importance in this world. I can name them for you and I can promise that I shall do everything in my power to bring them about.

11

"First, we must continue and even *increase* our friendly, conciliatory posture toward our friends in those countries among the major powers on the other side of the world. Our very survival depends on it! Second, we must do all we can to dismantle the military-industrial complex within the establishment and see that once and for all our boys will never again have to go to war.

"Our current president has already done a great deal toward bringing about the third important goal. We must show our support for efforts to end this foolish playing as Space Ranger. God never meant for us to go into space. That's His domain. Yet, we have this monstrous, money-gobbling boondoggle that, in the final analysis, comes down to nothing more than a lot of small boys playing with toy rockets. Let the Russians waste their resources exploring space. We need that money for vitally important social engineering projects; for enhancing the lifestyle of those unfortunates who must exist on welfare; for the establishment of a national health care program. And I intend to get it for those worthy causes.

"The fourth goal is one that touches each and every one of you. We must end the terror in our streets, along the quiet by-ways of our rural districts and in the dwindling wilderness areas of our great nation. I mean, we have to bring an end to the barbarous cruelty of hunting and get firearms out of the hands of the people! It's a proven fact that guns cause crime. A man with a gun in his hand is an irresponsible animal . . . a disaster looking for a place to happen. Guns, guns, guns . . . we have a nation overflowing with them and the tragedy they cause makes headlines every day. Guns have never

12

done one good thing for this country and they never will!"

"Tell that to George Washington and the Continental Army, you Red creep!" a voice from the back of the crowd yelled. A few nervous titters followed, mixed with some scattered applause.

"Ah! I see the NRA goon squad has arrived in the nick of time. Well, gentlemen, I have no desire to debate the obvious with you. All I can say is that there's plenty of barbeque, watermelon, and beer. Help yourselves and stay awhile. Maybe you'll see the light."

Taking their cue from the speaker, the band struck up again and Andy Wells moved to the edge of the platform to greet well-wishers. Starting down the steps, hands out, he grasped eager palms extended to him while the crowd cheered.

The sound of the music acted, in its turn, as a cue for Art Belman. Sucking in a deep breath he expelled half of it, holding the rest while he waited a fraction of a second for the surge of his blood to slacken. The index finger of his left hand began taking up the nearly nonexistent slack in the feather-light, Timken trigger. The moment of his great performance had arrived.

Three quarters of the way across the nation, the Penetrator watched as a color television image dissolved from the newsroom set to a live coverage exterior. The voice of the commentator reached him filled with all the fervent tones of a dedicated convert.

"This is Harlow Renault at large, bringing you

another slice of Americana along our Highways and Byways. Over the past few months, as the primary elections have taken the forefront of the political scene, one race in particular has drawn national attention. This time we're not referring to the presidential race. The two-way contest in Alabama for the senatorial seat of incumbent Nelson Lemmon has been so hotly contested that it has brought our Highways and Byways cameras here to Riverfront Park in Montgomery to get a live view of real down-home campaigning.

"The more colorful of the candidates is Andrew Carver Wells. And I can truly tell you that if in pursuing the electioneering trail you have never before encountered a soul food campaign picnic you don't know what campaigning is all about. The entry of Wells into the contest has split the Democratic Party here in Alabama. Wells, whom his supporters frankly admit is a blatantly ethnic offering, has gathered tremendous support, including powerful members of the Central Committee. Not only has the president engaged in some backwoods stumping for Mr. Wells, but anomaly of all anomalies, the junior senator from Massachusetts has also endorsed his candidacy. For a Yankee . . . and a liberal one at that . . . to invade the conservative precincts of Southern bossism is an unheard-of event in politics. Nevertheless, according to the latest polls, Wells has gained by this maneuver. In the tradition of the head of his party, Mr. Wells seems to offer something for everyone while taking a hardline stand on issues he considers important."

On the TV screen, behind the commentator, Wells could be seen going through his speech, the gnawed-upon rib bone marking the rhythm of his

14

words. The Penetrator watched Wells—a moon-faced black man with the chubby cheeks and slightly pop-eyes of Idi Amin—with only mild curiosity. What he was saying could also be heard as Harlow Renault stepped out of the scene, turning his vast audience over to be regaled by Wells' words.

As the speech ended and the music came up, the Penetrator followed the action with casual indifference while Wells walked briskly to the steps leading from the platform and began shaking hands with many in the crowd. The rotund black politician had set his foot on the first step when he paused to do the Dap with an Afro-coiffed Negro youth. As they slapped palms and bumped elbows, a small hole appeared in Andy Wells' forehead and the back of his head exploded, showering those behind him with flesh, bone, blood, and bits of gray matter. The fatally wounded Wells seemed to totter backward a moment, then crumpled and leaned far forward. His knees gave way and he fell face first down the steps.

The crowd disintegrated into a welter of isolated individuals, faces blank, eyes glazed, mouths opened to release their first screams of incomprehension and fear. Police and security men scattered through the throng, many with sidearms drawn, others bellowing at the people to stay where they were. Harlow Renault appeared on camera, white faced and glassy eyed with horror. His voice choked as he tried to describe the scene.

"Oh, my God! They've shot him! They've killed him! This is the most awful thing I have ever seen. Andy Wells is down, blood . . . Oh, God, the blood everywhere. It's terrible, horrible. Oh, he's killed, killed. . . ." His image disappeared abruptly as the engineer in the master control room cut to the network's New York studio. The Penetrator came to his feet in the same instant.

Hurrying into the Intelligence Center, Mark punched Andy Wells' name and those of his opponents into the computer, calling for everything available on all three men, including the American People's Party candidate, Johnny Herter. He added a code for all data on power politics in Alabama and waited impatiently while the electronic brain ruminated. While it did, Mark thought over the reasons for his precipitous action.

The Penetrator didn't know Andy Wells. He didn't, from what he'd heard of the speech, think he'd like Wells if he did know him. And he definitely didn't like the politics the man espoused. But the cold-blooded murder of a public figure transcended personality and politics. The assassination of a candidate going about his lawful business was something the Penetrator liked even less and was determined to do something about.

Chapter 2
Profiles of a Politician

Only five cars occupied the large tarmac parking lot on Upper Wetumka Road in Montgomery, Alabama.

They nestled against one windowless wall of what had once been a Piggly-Wiggly supermarket, as though seeking companionship. A sixth vehicle entered the drive, a Mercedes phaeton limousine, which, as if to make clear the distinction in social class, remained aloof from the dust-and dent-afflicted commoners huddled in their cluster. A liveried chauffeur slid smoothly from behind the wheel and opened the rear door. A strikingly handsome man stepped from the air-conditioned comfort of the plush auto and walked briskly to a side entrance of the building.

Johnny Herter had class as well as money, which had made him an attractive figure for the American People's Party to run for senator against the two major parties. Despite the traditional difficulty for a third party candidate to win the election, the organizers of the APP felt they had a good thing in Johnny Herter.

Contrary to what logic would seem to dictate, the political pundits had long ago decided that the image of a "grass roots" populist candidate should not include dirt under the nails and a blue collar. He should, in fact, be at least a millionaire, blessed with charismatic charm and good looks and the worldly-wise aplomb of a jetsetter. Herter met these criteria with a little something extra.

He had begun his rise to his present postition of wealth and influence with a chain saw in the pine forests of Tennessee. Through shrewd dealings and equally hardheaded poker playing, Herter had elevated himself from the sawdusty existence of a lumberjack to that of the owner of a vast and valuable plantation in northeastern Alabama, which produced cotton, cattle, and peanuts. By his own criteria, Johnny Herter was an honest man.

Once he had given it, he rarely, if ever, went back on his word. His adherence to ethical and moral principals, though, could hardly be gauged by a rigid yardstick. Herter's conduct along those lines could better be compared to a slide rule. Whatever benefit came his way, no matter by what means, he accepted with the casual attitude of its being his due, as though he were some feudal lord of times past. Not even his entrance into politics, under the radical Left banner of the American People's Party, seemed a contradiction. Herter explained it as a natural outgrowth of his "proletarian origins." As he entered the Montgomery campaign headquarters of the APP on this particular day, though, his rugged origins were well concealed beneath the rich cloth of an expensively tailored, pearl-gray, three-piece suit.

Inside, a steady hum of voices came from a battery of telephone solicitors installed in a double rank along one wall. Herter strode through the bustle of campaign workers to what had once been the

18

supermarket manager's office. Once past that door, soundproofing provided refuge from the noise on the floor outside. A smile flashed whitely on Johnny's face as he took in the men assembled for this meeting.

Porter Carson, face pinched from mild but incessant pain, sat in his wheelchair near the central table. His bloodless lips and pale complexion were made whiter still by overhead fluorescent lights. He gave a curt nod of greeting. Horse-faced Dave Guthrie, who held on to a thick sheaf of papers, beamed enthusiastically at the candidate. The other two present, Albert Fields, and Morton Sutter, were not part of the campaign structure. Instead, they represented large independent coal mining companies. Guthrie began before Herter had time to take a chair.

"It's going great, Johnny. We've reports from nearly half the state. Wells' supporters are switching to our team in wholesale lots. In many cases they're bringing their entire precinct machinery along with them."

"That *is* good news, Dave." Herter turned his attention to the balding, gray-haired figure of Porter Carson. "Didn't we tell you it would all work out the way we planned?"

"I'm reserving judgment until we find out if the FBI is going to take an interest in Andy Wells' killing."

Ignoring the crippled man's sour commentary, Johnny Herter spoke to Guthrie again. "What about here in town?"

"Chisholm, Highland Garden, Oak Park, Cloverdale, and downtown are all sewed up. Same for Green Acres and Brentwood. Our big problems are with Highpoint Estate, Pecan Grove, Johnstowne, and College Grove, and of course the military types around Gunter Air Force Base. These phone solicitors, using the voter registration lists, are doing a great job."

"Okay. Let's drop politics for a while. Al, Mort, I don't think it's wise for you to be here. Time is short enough before the primary and we're living in a fish bowl as a result. That's not hyperbole, it's a fact. The press is in here all the time. If any of them recognize you two from the coal mining scandal, we could be in for a lot of embarrassing questions."

"Look. All we wanted to do is show you the map on that new piece we're working on. It's right behind Pine Grove on that government land, so you should be aware of the extent of operations. With your plantation being used as a cover, you stand to make a good deal more money than on past mining ventures."

"We could have gone over this tonight at Pine Grove. You're coming, aren't you?"

"Of course. We're here now, so why don't we give it a look?"

"All right, all right. Let's make it quick and then . . . go out the back way, okay boys?"

Albert Fields flushed red at Johnny's suggestion. Then he unrolled a strip of blueprint paper, placing it on the table, weighted down by overflowing ashtrays. His finger stabbed at an elongated series of closely spaced lines that indicated a ridge.

"Here's the main coal vein. It runs for about two miles, better than ten feet thick. We don't yet know how far it extends into the face of this ridge, but it is well worth working. As you can see, the north boundary of your plantation, Pine Grove, is only a quarter mile from the ridge. From the quality of the coal, we estimate we can take out about two hundred thousand dollars' worth a day. Now . . ." A discreet knock on the room's only door ended conversation. Fields re-rolled his map and placed it in a cardboard tube.

"What is it?" Dave Guthrie inquired through the closed panel.

"It's important, Mr. Guthrie. I need to speak to you and Johnny."

"All right, Phil. Come on in."

Phyllis Landers entered, smiling, her eyes alight with the importance of the news she bore. "Mr. Guthrie, Johnny . . . there are two gentlemen outside who want very much to talk with you. They're from Andy Wells' party state central committee, but they wish to remain anonymous."

Herter and Guthrie exchanged exuberant, boyish grins. "If you gentlemen will excuse us?" When Fields and Sutter had filed out of the room, Herter continued. "Okay, Phil, show them in."

Despite the willingness of a large segment of the media to cooperate in exploiting Johnny Herter's rags-to-riches success story and the phenomenal swelling of his ranks by those coming into the fold from among the party stalwarts of the late Andy Wells, one reporter remained unimpressed by the great hope of Alabama liberals. For all Johnny Herter's insistence that he never forgot his humble origins, that his sympathies lay with the workers and those ground into oppressive poverty, Ed Merril didn't believe it for a moment. Ed suspected that Herter far too greatly enjoyed the luxury and privilege that came with wealth and power. Herter, he maintained, had long forgotten the callused hands and bulging forearms that came from running a chain saw.

Ed came by his opinion legitimately. For the past five years he had been a top investigative reporter for *Floodlight*, a Washington, D.C.-based weekly news digest that purported to publish all the news the liberal press ignored. Ed had exposed the now-famous Cocaine Connection. It was he who had revealed the facts and figures that implicated the family of Panama's Marxist dictator, Omar Torillos, in the international drug business. For the past year, since the revelation of illegal coal mining on public lands—a rip-off that, according to CBS News, had cost the American people more than $65 million—his attention had been centered on Johnny Herter. Herter's social and financial association with several executives of coal companies, suspected but as yet unindicted for the grab of publicly owned coal, were well known to Ed Merril. This factor, though, constituted only a small portion of the case Ed had been building. So, while Johnny Herter listened with eager anticipation to the purpose of the visit by state committeemen, Ed wrangled over the content of his first *Floodlight* article on the candidate.

"Listen to this, Joe," Ed Merril said to one of his legmen. He swung away from the heavy plank counter that served as his desk in the well-lighted den of his home. " 'While no direct connection can be made between Herter and God's Blood, wherein the flow of supervision or finance runs from the candidate to the rock group, the reverse situation is easily shown. So far two rock concerts have been held in Alabama, the proceeds of which went into the coffers of Herter's campaign. Duce Wilde, leader of the controversial God's Blood rock group, has frequently been photographed with Herter. On one occasion Herter posed with his arm around the shoulders of Wilde, while the band leader presented him with a check for thirty-five thousand dollars.

" 'Followers of the rock scene, and many among the general public, are aware that the group has been the subject of recent investigations into the illegal narcotics trade. Three members of the band are under indictment for possession of narcotics for sale, and transportation of narcotics interstate for the purpose of sale. Other indictments are pending on charges ranging from conspiracy to murder. In the name of entertainment, God's Blood presents a blending of sexual symbolism, irreligious lyrics, and raunchy, atonal music, delivered at a deafening roar that defies conversation. In the past, candidate Herter has frequently attended their concerts, giving lavish praise to their "creative genius."

" 'On this surface evidence alone, the first question that should occur to a serious-minded person is: "Do we want this sort of man for a senator?" Leaving the rock world for a moment, we can clearly see that Herter's preoccupation with God's Blood isn't the only chapter in the story of the strange people who surround the candidate. There is, for instance, the endless stream of kooks, radicals, and financial advisers of questionable background—such as Birmingham's Dave Guthrie—with whom Herter has staffed his campaign organization.' " Ed interrupted his reading to insert instructions.

"This is where we're going to have to concentrate our efforts for the time being, Joe. We can't prove that Herter got anything out of that coal rip-off, or

23

that he is even aware of it. But this collection of weirdos is proof of where Herter is really coming from. Eventually all these bits and pieces will fall into their proper places. As it is, I've already got the direction I'm going to go in this lead article.

"Ask yourself this: How does this mob of creeps, these drug-pushing hippie musicians, these bomb-throwing radicals, slippery fixit-type fund raisers, all the rest, fit with the image of a Born Again Christian?"

"Aren't you hitting below the belt in picking on Herter's religion?"

"Not if there's an inconsistency, Joe. And we won't be pointing any fingers at his religion, but at him. The angle is: Has Herter really experienced a spiritual rebirth, or is he cynically appealing to the religious convictions of the electorate? How can Herter reconcile his praise as 'creative genius' of such lyrics as: 'Let's get down together baby, fuck, fuck, fuck!' with the moral standards of other Born Again types? Of course we can't use that example in *Floodlight*. The readers would crucify us . . . no, more likely they'd lynch us. But, sticking to the point, that's the way I want to handle this first article.

"I have it on the most reliable authority that the wild orgies Herter throws at Pine Grove are still going on. Oh, they're much more discreet than before his emergence as a candidate, but there are still plenty of bare butts and boobies swinging around the pool to satisfy the most jaded appetite. The way I get it, one of Herter's Playboy-style parties is going on tonight. I think I'll slip out there with some high speed film and get photos to back up my copy."

"Hadn't I better do that for you, Ed? Herter has some good security and if you got caught, it'd be a trespassing rap for sure. Me? Nobody knows my connection with you or *Floodlight*. I could just be a Herter backer wanting some candid shots of the great man. That way we'd not tip them off in advance."

"No problem, Joe. I can handle it. Besides, I've lived and breathed Johnny Herter for a year now and I want to be the one to slap him back in place. I'll drive up there this afternoon. By tomorrow we should have one hell of a good start on the story."

Chapter 3
Caligula Revisited

Acid rock blared in discordant and disjointed phrases from weatherproof speakers installed under the eaves near the huge pool at Johnny Herter's Pine Grove Plantation. The voices raised in conversation and laughter, though many, seemed muted overall. An even dozen heads bobbed in the swimming pool while the wavelets broke rays from the underwater lights into gems of eye-dazzling brightness on the surface. One lovely female form swam to the edge and climbed out.

Entirely nude, showing not the least bit of self-consciousness, she walked with long-legged, hip-swaying grace to the diving boards. Climbing the chromed rungs of a ladder, she poised herself on the high board. Several pairs of eyes, displaying various degrees of interest and lust, watched her performance. Stretching languidly, the girl lay down and spread wide her legs, beginning to pantomime an act of intercourse. Her gyrations grew in violence until reaching a point of frenzied abandon, that the audience easily interpreted as her approach to climax. At that point, she gave a great cry of ecstasy and fell from the board, sending up a resounding splash. Expressing their appreciation with shouts and applause, the revelers quickly sought out other diversions.

A nude couple lay on a pale green nylon chaise, one atop the other, engaging in mutual oral copulation. As their exertions increased the frame creaked warningly and a crowd began to gather. Several spectators made bets as to which one would get off first. Three strips of the nylon webbing tore with stuttering shrieks and gales of laughter rose in the night air as the tubular aluminum frame collapsed, dumping the participants onto the green indoor-oudoor carpeting beneath, ending their endeavors cruelly short of completion. The onlookers drifted on, some diving into the pool, others wandering off to seek new activitites, a few, walking hand-in-hand, headed toward the spacious plantation house. From the poolside bar, Johnny Herter observed it all with amused silence.

"Here's your Chablis, Mr. Herter," the bartender voiced with diffidence.

"Thank you, Henry." Herter accepted the glass of white wine and sipped sparingly. He lowered the stemmed crystal as Dave Guthrie approached.

"Enjoying yourself?"

"I always do, Dave. Bunny's as great as ever. She did her 'I'm-gettin-laid-on-the-diving-board' routine."

"I saw it. Are you sure it's wise to be holding this bash?"

"Hell, Dave, you designed the security system. We're safer here than the president is in the White House. Besides, after playing Goodie-Two-Shoes for weeks on end, a guy's gotta blow it off sometime." Herter brushed an elegant linen handkerchief at his running, slightly reddened nose. "Uh . . . look,

Dave, I've got to take care of something important. I'll get back with you, okay?"

Guthrie frowned. "You snorting again, Johnny?"

"C'mon, Dave. I've gotta have some fun, right?"

"You keep this up and you'll have to start wearing makeup for TV appearances."

"So what? It never hurt the Man from Plains's clean-cut, American-boy image did it?" Turning away, Herter headed toward the house.

Beyond one set of sliding glass doors that gave access to the poolside area, Johnny Herter entered a plush and lavishly furnished living room. Antiques dating from the ante-bellum South mingled well with a massive, modern four-piece sectional, a d'Arcy glass coffee table, and a wall filled with stereo equipment. Soft murmurs of mutual appreciation came from two embracing couples making use of the divided couch. Herter crossed the room and mounted the three Lextran-carpeted steps, turning into a narrow hallway.

Doors along the hall gave access to various guest rooms. Johnny smiled with genuine appreciation and his pulse quickened as he thought of the manner in which these cubicles had been furnished for the party. A muffled cry of pleasure-pain came from behind the first closed door. An assortment of whips, chains, leather thongs, and other implements of restraint had been placed there for those who were into the leather and bondage scenes and other S-M games.

The *pièce de résistance* was a large, X-shaped wooden crucifix that could be adjusted to the desired angle by ropes through pulley in the ceiling. If he'd read the signals properly, earlier in the evening, Johnny mused, Larry Jay and Peter Nichols of

God's Blood would be the ones currently putting the equipment to passionate use.

Low-level, blood red light flooded through the next open doorway. Along with it came the rhythmic squeaking of bedsprings. A quick glance revealed to Johnny the identities of the occupants.

Ah, the good Reverend Tisdale, Johnny mused, *rutting in proper missionary position atop that preteen groupie he brought. Hell of a guy to be in charge when you get born again.* But one had to give the Reverend Joshua Tisdale credit. He had "saved" many socially and politically prominent persons. Not the least among them, Johnny conceded cynically, himself. Maybe the good Reverend was conducting another conversion. Might be he was trying to drive the devil out the same way he'd slithered in. Johnny stopped at the entrance to the master bedroom.

Inside, Johnny went to the adjoining bathroom and returned with a glassine envelope containing a white powder. He dumped the contents onto the glass top of a wrought-iron lamp table. Using a razor blade, he divided the cocaine into four relatively equal lines. From his money clip he took a hundred dollar bill and rolled it into a tube. Seating himself, he bent low over the preparation and inserted the paper tube into one nostril. Inhaling deeply, he snorted up the coke, two lines to each nasal passage. Then he leaned back in the chair and sighed in contented relaxation. A knock at the door snapped open drooping eyelids.

"Go the hell away," Herter managed to get out.

The door opened, admitting Dave Guthrie and another top aide. "We've got to talk, Johnny. That is, if you haven't snorted yourself into oblivion."

30

A crooked, vacuous smile creased Herter's handsome face at a lopsided angle. He waved a rubber-armed gesture of dismissal. "Some other time, Dave. Gimme an hour."

"I mean *now*. Andy Wells' campaign manager and some of his money people are outside. They want to discuss details with you."

"Shit! They didn't see this . . . this orgy, did they?"

"No. I brought them in the back way."

"Good boy. I can always rely on you, Dave. Uh . . . tell 'em . . . tell 'em I'm indisposed," he snickered at the word. "I'll see them in my office in half an hour."

"I think I can hold them that long. I'll put them in the office, build some drinks. That ought to do. But, this thing is important, Johnny. We didn't have Belman do his number on Wells simply to get rid of a loud-mouthed nigger. These guys are coming to us now, like we wanted. If we expect the plan to work, it means you have to be nice to them. And that means get off and stay off the coke."

"The plan will work, Dave, whether I'm nice to those stuffed-shirt sonsofbitches or not. Who the hell else can they go to?"

Guthrie frowned. Unlike many users under the influence of alcohol and cocaine Johnny Herter became aggressive and abusive. And over the past year, Guthrie had noticed subtle changes in Herter's straight personality that intensified his aggressive attitudes when snorted up. If that continued, they'd have a hard time controlling him once elected to the Senate. His periods of depression and savage temper were becoming more frequent. Next thing they knew, he might smash hell out of something and

31

claim he'd been attacked by a rabbit. Dave decided to be placating.

"Okay, Johnny. No problem dealing with them if you say so. We do have one real pisser, though. I'd better let Tim explain it. He's the one who brought it to me."

Tim James revealed his information in sparing words. "Remember that creep reporter who did those articles for that Rightist rag, *Floodlight*?"

"Yeah. Ed Merril, right?"

"That's the one, Johnny. He lives near Gadsen, darn near in your own backyard. Word is he's snooping around again. My source says he's planning an exposé series for *Floodlight* in the event you make it into the general election. He's also going to put some things into the two Montgomery papers, the Birmingham sheets, and other key cities over the next few days before the primary. None of it will help you at all."

Johnny Herter scowled, his face blooming red with sudden anger. "That bastard! If he can't be bought off and he keeps up this nosing around, Dave, something . . . aaah . . . er, permanent, might have to be done."

Ed Merril couldn't believe what he saw. This was too good to trust to his eyes alone. He kept swinging and focusing the long lens on his motor-drive Olympus OM-1, tapping the shutter release in three frame bursts, to get assurance of cover shots.

There, by the bar near the pool. A good shot of Jerry Dubinsky, the bomb-throwing Leftist radical from the Weather Underground who did time for blowing up that laboratory. And there beside him,

Shirley O'Shane, the one-time Hollywood biggie who'd been donating so much money and talent lately to Red causes. There's that fruit judge from California, cruising all the young guys around the pool. Ooops! He's zeroed in on that little blond kid. Hell, he can't be over fifteen. No wonder Hizonor is so anti-gun. He's probably afraid he'll grope the wrong crotch some night and get blown away.

Ed's camera whirred three times, recording the chicken queen jurist placing his hand firmly on the inside surface of the youngster's thigh. *Too bad* Floodlight *won't run that one*, Ed thought. *Although I hear the faggot's being nominated for the federal bench. Maybe they can use it after all. So this is how the great Born Again Christian, Johnny Herter, enjoys his spare time*, Ed wondered as he recorded the host's reaction to the collapsing chaise longue. Ed changed positions again, to avoid the roving security patrol, and to get more coverage on Herter with the orgiastic goings-on in the background.

From another angle, Ed Merril got Johnny in the same frame with Jerry Dubinsky and photoed his brief conversation with Dave Guthrie. When Johnny departed toward the house, Ed moved again, barely escaping detection by the two-man teams of guards. His wanderings took him along the outside of the bedroom wing of Herter's large house. He listened to the varied sounds of sexual pleasure coming from different rooms. Could Herter be in one of them? Then a light came on in a larger window at the far end of the structure. Hiding his camera from the view of another pair of security men, Ed headed that way.

Ed slipped quietly up to the window, which stood partially open. Light curtains somewhat diffused the details of images beyond, but Merril could clearly tell what he saw. He arrived in time to watch Johnny cut his cocaine and administer it. The OM-1 *wheezed* off frame after frame of fast ASA 400 film, until Herter settled back in his chair. Merril had stepped into an investigative reporter's dream. It also created a problem. Should he let *Floodlight* have exclusive use of this irrefutable proof of Johnny Herter using illegal drugs, earning himself a great deal of money in the process and enhancing his national reputation? Or should he act for the greater good of the people of Alabama by taking the photos to the elections commission and local authorities? He moved away from the window, pondering his dilemma while he changed the self-contained, 250-frame film backs. The sound of arguing voices brought him back.

Ed's departure to cover the metallic clicks of the change in film backs and mull over his indecision prevented him from hearing about Art Belman's contribution to Johnny Herter's campaign, though he did get back in time to listen in on the discussion involving himself. Herter's ominous comment about doing something permanent was followed by an objection from Dave Guthrie.

"You aren't thinking of using Belman again, are you?"

"I don't know what I mean until we find out how many local people are taking this Merril puke seriously. On the other hand, that don't sound like a bad idea," Johnny added with grim glee. "Rat-ta-tat-tat, blow his ass away."

34

Shaken by hearing Herter's obvious pleasure at contemplating his murder, Ed hurried away. He walked in shadow down the long drive until he came to a cattle guard. This, he knew, was the inner security fence. He waited until a car came along and went through the gate with it, leaving no trace of his own movement. Another hundred yards along the curving lane, he crouched in a clump of bushes for fifteen minutes while two roving patrols met and talked for a short while. Sweating heavily, although the night air was cool, Ed watched them anxiously until both teams were out of sight. Then he sprinted through the open main gate and down the road. In a few minutes he reached his car, which was parked along a dark side road, and started toward his home outside distant Gadsden.

One issue had settled itself. He could never get the material to *Floodlight* in time to come out before the primary election. He'd develop the film and see what he could use for the local papers.

Chapter 4
Hit Man in Hiding

Mark Hardin arrived in Guntersville, Alabama, three days after Belman killed Andy Wells. He sought a man about whom he had only a marginal description and a name. Art Belman.

Belman's name had come from the computer along with several others reputed to be involved with the southern branch of Syndicate operations. A stop in Atlanta had provided the Penetrator with a pair of reliable informants who had indicated that Belman could be the man who shot down the senatorial candidate. They also told Mark that Belman liked Guntersville Lake as a playground.

The Atlanta-based hit man filled contracts for the Andropopolous combine in Georgia, Tennessee, and Alabama, then cooled off among the anonymous crowds at the various lake resorts. Although all sources indicated that Belman would be an ideal suspect, none of them offered any speculation as to why or by whom the hit might have been ordered. Finding Belman and learning this information from him wouldn't be an easy proposition, Mark conceded as he drove through the streets of Guntersville. He had been aware of that difficulty from the moment he arrived in Alabama.

On the day before, Mark had landed at Dannelly Field in Montgomery after getting an aerial view of the site where Wells had been assassinated. He wanted to spend some time "getting the feel" of the scene. From the air he had spotted the location from which the killer must have fired his fatal shot. It, and Riverside Park, were cordoned off by police. He couldn't gain much here, he decided. He rented a car and from his light aircraft Mooney 201 had taken two identical metal suitcases. One contained clothes, the other an assortment of weapons that could easily get him half a dozen federal raps for firearms and explosives violations.

His eighteen-and-a-half-inch-long SS-IV Sidewinder submachine gun rested in the center of the large valise, its tubular-metal, telescoping stock retracted against the rear of the receiver. Nestled in two parallel lines of depressions in the foam rubber lining that resembled an egg carton were half a dozen M-27 fragmentation grenades, their smooth outer casings a dull green color, and an equal number of pale blue-green ovoids, the yellow stripe around their middles indicating white phosphorus. Disassembled, the Mossberg M500 ATP 8S riot gun barely fit the confines of the case. The remaining space was taken up with silencers, extra ammunition, and pockets holding his extension barrel Colt Commander, a spare Star PD and a second model of Ava, the Penetrator's CO_2-powered dart pistol. It made a heavy load, but once he'd located Belman, Mark wanted to be sure of having the means of dealing with the killer. Toward that end, the Penetrator had but a single lead. One of his informants had given the Penetrator the name of a hotel Belman favored in Guntersville. Mark reached the front entrance of the hostelry at the same time Andy Wells' funeral began in Montgomery.

"Mr. Belman, sir? No. He's not registered here at this time." The desk clerk had the condescending, prissy manner generally affected by employees of far more lavish establishments than the Hillcrest Hotel.

"Has he been here recently?" the Penetrator pressed.

"Well now, sir, I'm not at liberty to . . . aaah . . ." The figures 2 and 0 in white-on-green appeared magically between the Penetrator's outspread fingers. "Let me check." Spinning the reel of the large registry index, the clerk stopped at one oblong white form.

"Now isn't that a coincidence? Mr. Belman was here until this morning." The clerk plucked the twenty-dollar bill from between Mark's fingers as deftly as the Penetrator had first made it appear.

'He leave any indication of where he would be going?"

"Hmmm. No . . . I don't see any notation of advance reservations. I'm afraid I can't recall anything . . . aaaah." Another twenty materialized in the place vacated by the first. "Though he *did* say something about getting in a little fishing up around Scottsboro."

"Thank you, you've been a great help."

The Penetrator ran into a traffic jam at the intersection of State 79 and 35. Turning right he crawled along through the small city of Scottsboro until he reached the center of town. There he saw the reason for the inordinate amount of traffic in a resort community of no greater size than this.

Barter Day, Scottsboro's century-old tradition, came each first Monday of the month. Mark had picked the busiest possible morning to be hunting a killer. Quilts, axe handles, produce, home-baked goods, and items from a blacksmith's forge-covered tables, portable stalls, and the tailgates of pickup trucks scattered about Courthouse Square. The sound of spirited bargaining filled the air as locals and tourists sought to swap or wrangle a good price on various items. Mark turned onto the first side street leading away from the congested area and sought a place to lay out his plans.

Art Belman pushed back the plate that now contained only two fish skeletons and a small dab of hominy grits. His breakfast, or more accurately brunch, had been brought up by room service. He patted his stomach and looked at the two men seated in the room.

"Now that's livin'. Rainbow trout, eggs, biscuits, and grits for breakfast. Who could ask for more?"

"I hate fish," a carrot-haired, broad-shouldered man offered with feeling. "Gimme hotcakes and sausage any day."

Belman found interest in this gastronomic debate. "Never. They lay in your stomach like lead, slow down your reactions, and stultify your mental processes, Gil."

Gilbert Blessing twitched his arm and rolled his shoulder in a blurr of motion. A Browning 9mm Highpower appeared in his hand. "I just had a double stack, sausage, and two eggs. Didn't slow me any."

"Okay, okay. I'm impressed." Blessing's exhibition of gunhandling skill reminded Belman of his current pet gripe. "I still don't see why I have to be saddled with you guys. I can take care of myself."

"From what I've heard, I'm sure you can. But the man who hired you and us says we stay with you until you leave the country. Once you're in the Bahamas for that extended vacation, our job is done."

"So I'm stuck with four baby sitters until the payoff gets here. Where are the other guys?"

Gil Blessing indicated one of two doors leading to the bedrooms of the suite. "They're sleepin' so they can take the night trick again."

"Then, I suppose, whether you like fish or not, you're stuck with me. I feel like seeing how the pickerel are biting."

Blessing made a face. "You're not going to *eat* them after you catch 'em, are you?"

"Hell, yes. We'll pull into one of those coves at the state park and fix chow on an outdoor fireplace. You know, Gil, if you ate more fish and less pork you'd feel a lot better." At Belman's return to the original subject, Blessing's mouth twisted into a grimace as though he'd bitten into something extremely foul. "I'm serious. All that cholesterol in heavy meat. You'll wind up with clogged arteries, high blood pressure, maybe have a heart attack or get cancer from all those chemicals they feed livestock these days. But not me. I eat fish."

"Yeah. And rice and collards and grits and . . . and *bran* for God's sake. That stuff's for pickaninnies."

Amused, Belman replied in a tone of virtuous superiority. "Besides being a dietary oaf, Gil, you're a bigot. But let's get this fishing trip under way. Call the marina and tell them we want a bass boat for the day. The tackle and poles are in my car."

The second bodyguard, who had pointedly avoided the conversation so far, looked up from the sports page of the newspaper he had been studiously examining. "Am I going, too?"

"You are," Gil told him in a "misery-loves-company" tone.

Three hours and not a trace of Belman, the Penetrator thought sourly as he walked into the parking lot at the marina. There were only so many places Belman could be staying and only a limited number of others he could have gone. Mark couldn't see a professional killer haggling over the price of a "Bow-tie" or "Wedding Ring" pattern quilt, so he had crossed the Barter Day gathering off his list. But Belman had come here to fish, so the marina had been included. As he headed toward the short flight of wooden steps leading to the dock, Mark's eyes automatically took note of the parked cars.

Wait a minute! One of the informants in Atlanta had told the Penetrator that Belman drove a Mazda RX-VII. There one sat, the same particular metallic blue color as Art Belman's. Mark gave the car a quick going over, but found nothing to verify his suspicion. Even so, the hunch node in his brain vibrated with a certainty that he had at last found the illusive assassin. He quickened his pace as he headed toward the distant figures, fishing along the dock.

The Penetrator altered his gait when he arrived on the pier. Ambling casually among the fishermen, he determined that Art Belman was not one of them. He spent a few moments gazing out across the wide lake for the purpose of seeming unhurried.

When even the most casual notice of his presence ceased, he strode toward the marina office.

"Oh, you mean Mr. Benson. Carl Benson," the marina manager supplied when the Penetrator described Art Belman. "He and a friend rented a bass boat about an hour ago."

"I was supposed to meet them here"—*Who's Belman got along and why*? the Penetrator's thoughts ran while he continued making a small-talk explanation—"to go fishing. But all the crowd for Barter Day slowed me down. I'm sorry I missed them. Say, what I have to see him about is really important. Now that I lost out meeting him here, you wouldn't happen to know what hotel he's staying at, would you?"

"Sure do. It's right here on the boat rental receipt. He's at the . . . ah . . . Wheeler House."

A smile brightened Mark's face. "Thank you. I'll try to reach him there later." The Penetrator left, feeling better than he had in two days. Sometimes hard-to-obtain information came just that easy. It was a long-time tested and valued cop technique. Act a little dumb and confused, ask an obvious question, and get the expected answer. Mark hurried to his car and drove to the largest and most luxurious of Scottsboro's resort hotels.

All he needed was the right name, the Penetrator reflected as he walked under the white columnated portico of the Wheeler House. Art Belman had used an alias, a crude one, but sufficient that Mark's first visit to this hotel had failed to bring results. Now he simply asked for Mr. Carl Benson's room and was directed to Suite 238 on the second floor rear of the wing that slanted toward the lake. Climbing the wide, curving staircase, Mark checked his weapons, making sure he was ready for anything.

Too much damn noise. Pete Yates had never liked sleeping days and working nights. This present assignment, bodyguarding a guy who acted like a hood and talked half the time like a college professor, hadn't improved his humor any. He climbed from under the covers, listening to the soft snores of his partner, Jim Hammer, in the bed opposite. Padding on bare feet across the hardwood floor, he opened the door and entered the main room of the suite.

"What the hell?" The words were startled out of Yates as he looked up to see a man slipping quietly through what should have been a locked door.

Ava hissed softly, sending a tiny dart into the well-muscled flesh of Pete Yates' chest. The neurological agent induced nearly instant spasming that jerked the burly bodyguard off his feet and left him a quivering mass of uncoordinated meat that flopped on the floor until the mixture of Pentothal and M-99 took hold and Yates slumbered peacefully. The Penetrator crossed the carpet in swift, silent strides, making a brief examination of the fallen man. Then he opened the connecting door.

A quick check, including a glance into the bedroom on the opposite side of the sitting room, indicated that no one else was in the suite. Mark went back to wait out the approximate fifteen minutes he estimated the drugged man would sleep.

Jim Hammer, a highly experienced professional, had awakened instantly at the sound of Pete Yates'

muffled but startled expression. Jim heard his partner's body hit the floor and the scrabbling sounds of
his spasms. Instinct guided him to snatch up his
two-inch barreled .38 Detective Special and remain
quiet. When the twitching went on too long to be
Pete's death throes, Jim slid into his trousers and,
taking his shoes in his left hand, slipped quietly into
the hallway an instant before the Penetrator opened
the inside door. While sounds of the search continued from the other side of the wall, Jim waited anxiously.

When quiet returned, he reentered the bedroom
and retrieved the rest of his clothes. He finished
dressing in the hall. Logic told him that from the
manner in which Pete had been taken out and the
swift search with nothing disturbed or taken, they
weren't dealing with an ordinary hotel burglar.
Reinforcements, he felt, were definitely called for.

Paragon Security. Hmmm. To occupy his time,
the Penetrator searched the unconscious man's clothing. In a wallet, in the pocket of a pair of trousers
folded over a chair in the bedroom, he found an ID
card giving Yates' name and employer. He also
found a state private investigator's ticket, driver's license, and Master Charge in the same name. Too
much cover for an out-of-town hood. This Pete
Yates must be legitimate. Even so, when Yates
came around, Mark's first question came hard and
direct.

"If you're not from the Syndicate in Atlanta, one
of Andropopolous' soldiers, what are you doing
looking after his number-one hit man?"

Pete Yates gave back a blank, innocent look.

"What the hell did you do to me? If this has something to do with that Atlanta Syndicate mob I don't want anything to do with it."

The Penetrator reached out and popped Yates soundly on the left cheek with an open palm. "You didn't answer my question, chum. What are you doing bird-dogging Art Belman?"

Anger coruscated in Pete's eyes, but he made no immediate move. Licking dry lips, he gave a sullen response. "Belman? Who is that? We're bodyguarding for a guy named Carl Benson."

"We? How many of you?"

"That's something I don't think I'm going to tell you."

Pain flowered in exquisite abundance from the nerve center under one hinge of Yates' jaw. With his interrogator extended outward, off balance, Pete decided the time had come to make his move. He lunged with cobra quickness, only to find the world spinning as he hurtled into the air, turning over once to land, ass-over-elbows, on the nubby upholstered couch. Hell, he hadn't even seen the guy so much as twitch and here he was, heels against the wall and head bent until his chin ground into the hair on his chest. He rolled his eyes at the sound of a muffled footstep. The big-chested, dark-skinned man stood over him, a faintly contemptuous smile on his full lips.

"We haven't time to do this the slow way." The Penetrator bent down, drawing up one pants cuff. His action revealed a black pouch, held in place by a wide, Velcro-lined band, from which he took a small hypodermic syringe and a slim vial. "So we do it the easy way."

Pete Yates pulled forcefully away from the needle

as the Penetrator leaned toward him to locate a vein in the arm. It did the man no good.

"It's only Pentothal. You'll get drowsy, tell me all I want to know, and then sleep it off."

Twenty-five minutes later, the Penetrator felt satisfied that he had learned everything Pete Yates could tell him. Paragon Security Service of Birmingham was apparently a legitimate agency, although frequently given to working in the gray areas of legality. Pete and his three fellow operatives, Gil Blessing, Jim Hammer, and Ted Sterling, had been assigned to act as bodyguards for a man they knew as Carl Benson. Yates said a tall, scrawny, horse-faced man who didn't give his name hired them, paying cash for a six-day stint and giving them a credit card made out to the David Felder Foundation to cover expenses. Okay, so it didn't wash.

The Penetrator went back through it again, after that first story. This time he elicited a slightly different version of Paragon's business, and of the nature of its employees. "Did you really take a job from a man who wouldn't give his name and gave you a credit card belonging to as world-famous an organization as the Felder Foundation?"

"Well," Pete mumbled. "The . . . the agency done work for him before. And with the type of clients we usually handled, all the guys figured it was better . . . not to ask personal questions."

"Tell me about the other members of your team."

Pete Yates frowned in drugged contemplation, seemed to drift off. Mark pinched the flesh of his right arm. "Unnh! Aaah. Oh, yeah . . . yeah. Jim, he's straight. Just likes PI work. But Gil . . . now him'n Sterling are something else. They've both done time in other states. Had to use political grease to get their concealed weapons permits an' PI tickets."

The Penetrator gave Yates a little extra Pentothal. "What about you?"

"I . . . I done a stretch for strongarming some guys for a loan company in Bayonne, New Jersey."

"Go on."

"I'm clean, man, clean. Oh . . . uh, there was . . . was that time charges on two counts of murder were dismissed for lack of evidence. The . . . boss had that Jersey DA on the pad."

The most revealing statement, though, came when Yates admitted that the previous night, when Benson-Belman had gotten fairly drunk in the hotel at Guntersville, he had hinted darkly at having something to do with blowing away that, as Yates put it, "loud-mouthed politician down in Montgomery." All in all, the Penetrator felt he had received more than his money's worth.

Yates was rousing from his drug stupor and Mark was preparing an injection to give him a long, deep sleep, when someone kicked open the door and took a shot at the Penetrator.

Chapter 5
Payoffs and Problems

The Penetrator catapulted backward in reflexive action even as the yellow-orange flame bloomed at the muzzle of Gil Blessing's Browning. The slug passed through empty space where Mark's right shoulder had been.

Doing a flip in the air, the Penetrator set himself to land on his feet. His right hand, which had dropped the syringe at the sound of splintering wood when the door crashed in, clawed for the Star PD in his Alessi shoulder while the left one fisted Ava. Mark hit the floor shooting.

A fat, blunt-nosed, 185-grain Federal JHP slug shattered Gil's sternum, clipped a groove in his aorta, and expended its energy crushing two vertebrae. Blood fountained into Gil's chest cavity, driving the air from his lungs with an inexorable pressure. His face took on a wondering, mildly painful expression as he dropped loose limbed to the expensive carpeting. Snapping his left arm seventy-five degrees to the left of his forward line of fire, Mark stroked Ava's trigger.

The .22-caliber dart pistol hissed briefly, sending a slim dart into Pete Yates' body as he tried to join the battle from his position on the couch. As Yates spasmed into unconsciousness, two more figures filled the doorway. Their guns blasted in a tight *ba-bang!* sequence, finding no solid target. The Penetrator was on the move again.

Mark executed a backward shoulder roll and began to scramble toward a set of French doors that led to an ornate, wood-banister balcony. One of the weapons behind him, a .380 auto he judged from a quick glance, spoke again and Mark felt a painful blow as the bullet smashed into his shoe, blowing away the heel. From beyond the two men in the doorway the Penetrator could faintly hear the shrill scream of a woman frightened by the sounds of the firefight. The Penetrator rammed into the fragile barrier, hearing glass and frame break noisily as the decorative latch gave way, spilling him out amidst the white wrought iron furniture.

Footsteps sounded in the room behind the Penetrator, who turned and fired three quick rounds through the ruined French doors. He heard a cry of pain and a strangled curse. Then Mark holstered his weapons momentarily and swung over the railing, thankful this suite was on only the second floor.

The Penetrator dropped five feet, landing on a broad canvas awning tautly stretched over a lattice framework of one-by-four slats, stoutly supported from below by a myriad of wrought iron posts. The covering shaded a veranda overlooking the swimming pool, tennis courts, and lake. He bounced once and lost little momentum as he slithered to the edge. Catching himself, Mark did a forward roll and extended his legs, letting go his grip as his feet swung perpendicular. The carpet-like lawn broke his final drop as startled exclamations rose from a clutch of elderly patrons enjoying an after-luncheon drink. Mark gained his feet again and sprinted toward the distant cover of a maintainance shed. Two shots sounded from above and behind him, one slug screaming off a steel net post on the tennis court to Mark's right. The sound added speed to his flight.

As the Penetrator ran for safety, one of the gunmen dashed into the hall and plunged down the stairs, appearing on the veranda amid the shouts of consternation from the now-frightened hotel guests. He dashed among the immobile staring waiters and gaping-mouthed patrons, angling to reach a point of ambush along Mark's escape route. Unaware of this threat, the Penetrator continued on his way, nearing the far end of the shed.

As the Penetrator rounded the building, trotting along the blind back side, his eyes scanned the hotel grounds, evaluating the best way to turn. From behind a large blooming lilac bush directly in Mark's path, Ted Sterling gulped to control his rapid breathing and concentrated on taking careful aim. He'd wait until the guy got so close he couldn't miss. When the Penetrator grew behind the sights until Sterling could clearly see the small white button in the center of Mark's light blue shirt, he began taking up the trigger slack.

Sterling's shot crashed loudly, rebounding off the clapboard building. But the bullet went far wide of its mark, *zinging* harmlessly high into the air. In the instant before the sear disengaged and released the hammer of Ted Sterling's pistol, a bullet entered the back of his head, scrambled his brains and killed him, irretrievably spoiling his aim. Reacting to the sound of the first shot, the Penetrator hit the ground, rolling to one side and whipping out his .45 auto.

Mark lay on the freshly cut, watermelon-smelling lawn listening to the brief thrashing in the lilac bush as Ted Sterling expired. *Who'd put in his oar*, he wondered. The Penetrator wasted little time pondering that question. He came to his feet with liquid smoothness. To his surprise, not a person was in sight. Keeping to a low crouch, he advanced.

As Mark rounded the lilac bush he got the answer—a slim, attractive, russet-haired young woman with strangely cat-like golden eyes stood spraddle-legged over Sterling's corpse. Her Detonics .45 auto was held rigidly at arm's length in a solid two-hand grip.

"Hell, he's already dead, Sam. You don't need to do that. But . . . how? Why? What are you doing here?"

Samantha Chase relaxed her pose, letting the arm holding her small, palm-sized pistol ease to her side. "I'll explain that later. Now let's get out of here before we have to answer a lot of embarrassing questions."

Ten minutes later, seated in the Penetrator's rental Caprice on a side road off State 35, Samantha Chase evaded Mark's question by a round-about approach to the subject in a casual, offhand tone. "Well, Captain Peters, there always seems to be a hell of a lot of shooting wherever you are."

"Uh . . . I'm not using that name now, Sam."

"I figured as much. Don't tell me you're down here on the same thing I am?"

"What's that?"

"The Andy Wells killing."

"What interest does NASA have with Andy Wells?"

"None. And . . . I'm not with NASA any more. We, uh, sort of, uh, had a parting of the ways.'

"Over my little trip into space?"

Yes. Partly that and other things. Going back to the same old routine became unbearably dull to me. I wanted something more, to be where the action was. And it seems I'd become too bloody-handed for so sedate and intellectual a civilian project as NASA. They suggested I resign and I jumped at the idea. I'm sort of freelancing it now."

"Why Wells?"

"That's where I figured the action would be. Besides, Andy Wells used to be active in the civil rights movement. I met him when I was stationed at the Huntsville space center not far from here. He and his organization were holding a demonstration there. Something about minority employment. We discussed rules for the protest march, things like that. I got to liking him . . . respecting what he stood for and all. That was before his far-Left swing when he started his campaign for senator. But dammit, no matter how off base his politics, people shouldn't be able to blow away a candidate and get away with it."

"I'll second that. How did that bring you here to Scottsboro?"

"Art Belman. From what I've learned so far, there may be some rather sinister political implications in this killing. The government must have the same opinion or Dan Griggs wouldn't have sent you down here."

I don't work for Griggs. I never have and I never will. I'm strictly a loner."

"Being on your own can sometimes get you in

deep cracks, as we just saw. Though I'll admit you handled yourself with your usual expertise."

"Hey, I was only trying to get some answers from a guy. These other people came busting in, they did all the shooting."

"Oh, sure they did. When I spotted you earlier today I decided to keep close on your tail. Seems like whenever the shooting starts, you're always in the center of the action. Or am I confusing you with that guy who goes around tossing out blue flint arrowheads and getting on the FBI's Most Wanted list?"

Mark Hardin felt a light brush of coldness, as though someone had opened the door to a walk-in freezer. The chilling sensation began in his throat and spread out and downward, delaying his reply. *Damn, too many people have learned facts about the Penetrator and suffered for it, some fatally. Now Sam, this bright, saucy, auburn-haired, competent—yeah, mustn't forget competent—helper from times past has to figure it out. Why does it always turn out to be the most valuable who pay the price for their knowledge?* The question was rhetorical and Mark had too often given himself the answer. He cleared his throat, seeking inspiration for diverting Samantha Chase's thrust, but doubting he could.

"Uh . . . Sam, where'd you get that wild idea?"

"C'mon, Peters, or whatever you're calling yourself now. I saw what you tossed into that room at the Holiday Inn in Clear Lake City. And later, the Penetrator is credited, or blamed, depending on your point of view, for hitting that TWIS intelligence center in D.C. on the same night you left my bed and arms to, as you put it, 'get a little action.' "

"Coincidence."

"Coincidence, bullshit. Let's quit futzing around. You *are* the Penetrator, I know it, and, sure as hell, Dan Griggs knows it. I don't care how many other people do. For all I know you could work for the Company."

"The CIA? Hardly. I told you I am a loner. That stands for the past, present, and *definitely* for the future."

"Touchy, aren't you? Look, obviously you and I are here for the same thing. You say you aren't doing it for DOJ, for the time being, I'll buy that. If we're both freelancing it, why not pool our knowledge and resources and get it on?"

In his desire to protect Sam from the danger that constantly surrounded the Penetrator, Mark decided to drop all pretense. "Okay. For the sake of argument, let's say I am who you think I am. That doesn't take away from my determination to be a lone operator. Hell, Sam, there must be half a hundred contracts out on the Penetrator. Except for the lowest creep and least-ranking street soldier in any organization I've ever gone after, those who survived want a piece of me in the worst way. I have a hard enough time watching my own back. Pretty as it is, I'd hate like hell to have to protect yours too."

"I can't cover my own ass? Ask those dudes in Mozambique. Where you been, Peters? This is the day of liberated womanhood. I'll take care of me and you take care of you."

"McDade. I'm using the name Stan McDade on this mission."

"Okay, Stan. I'm not one of Gloria's strident-voiced, bra-burning fanatics, but damnit, I don't need to be told how cute my butt is and how it needs protecting by some muscle-bulging male." Her remarkably colored eyes lost their greenish fire, mellowed to mischief-twinkling gold. "No putdown intended, McDade. You've got some mighty attractive bulging muscles. But . . . but . . . aawh, darn it, I need this case. If I can get to the bottom of who took off Andy Wells, I can reach national prominence as a PI. You know, like that guy in El Paso."

Mark though a moment, regretting as he did the ultimate decision he felt he must make. "All right. Truce at least. Let's share information to date. If . . . and I mean that, *if* you can come up with something you can do that is impossible for me to accomplish, then you're in all the way. Otherwise, you go your way and I go mine."

Sam Chase scowled, but she knew it was the best bargain she could strike.

"All right, let's lay out what we've got here," Johnny Herter said to the assembled men. A political strategy meeting had been in session for an hour at Herter's Pine Grove Plantation. The topic of conversation had come around to public officials and organizations bought off by the American People's Party and those willing to bribe them. When everyone's attention centered on him, Herter continued.

"Of course, here in Calhoun County we have Jed Barnes. Even though the Republicans managed to sneak in a man as sheriff, Barnes owes his job as chief deputy to the organization. We own him body and soul. We now have ranking police officers and sheriff's deputies in nearly every part of the state. We own outright six state senators and some twenty-five members of the legislature. We should be able

56

to elect five or six of our own in November. There's a scad more who owe us favors."

"Remember, Johnny, some of those favors have been called in for helping cover up the bootlegging of coal from public lands."

"Do they know that?" Johnny smiled at Dave Guthrie's negative shake of the head. "So it's your job, Dave, to make them think they haven't come near to paying off as yet. Now, there's three more mining companies that want a swing at that free coal. They'll pay us handsomely for protection. As long as we've got Jim Bolt in the attorney general's office, I think we can insure that.

"Then there's old man Andropopolous. He wants to bring in some of his mobile gamblin' rigs and run a string of whores in Alabama. Once I have the Democratic nomination for the Senate, there'll be enough people ridin' on my coat tails to insure local protection for the Greek's operation. Also, Jim can help along those lines. Though he keeps askin' for more money."

"He's worth it, Johnny."

"If you say so, Dave. Hey, we might offer him a little skim off the Atlanta Syndicate's revenue. That might take some of the pressure off our bank accounts."

"Good idea, Johnny. I'll ask Mr. Andropopolous about it." Marv Greene, the organization's liaison with the Syndicate, made a note while he spoke.

"You do that, Marv. There anything anyone else wants to bring up?"

"I do." Randall Seager, who had left the meeting earlier, entered the room. "We've got some big problems."

"What's that?"

"You ever heard of the Penetrator?"

"Sure," Johnny allowed. "Who hasn't?"

"It looks like he made a hit at Belman. I just heard from Pete Yates. A great big guy with a dark complexion and Indian nose jumped Pete at the suite in the Wheeler House. He questioned Yates under drugs, shot Gil and Ted—both of them are dead—and made his getaway. He left behind a pair of blue flint arrowheads.

"Pete and Jim have him safe and sound at another place. What are we going to do about the Penetrator nosing into our operation?"

"Nothing. At least for the time being." Johnny Herter looked at the surprised faces around the table. "Look, I know the reputation this guy has. The Penetrator is a mean sonofabitch. So what? He has nothing that connects Belman with us. Could be this crime-freak is after Belman because he works for Andropopolous. Maybe he's cleanin' up Atlanta." He turned to Dave Guthrie and Marv Greene. "That's something we'd better look into. Might be we'll need to make other arrangements for the vice concession.

"Now, as to the Penetrator. We sit and wait. If he surfaces again near anything we have a hand into, we deal with him quickly and finally. Could be we put Belman on it. Be neat if they wiped each other out, eh?"

"We have another problem, Johnny."

"Oh? Isn't one a day enough?" Studying the faces ranged toward him, Johnny realized he had been entirely too flip. He worked to regain ground. "Christ, I know it's rough, two guys get wasted and the Penetrator rampaging around us, but there's insulation enough between us and Belman to make

58

sure none of the shit falls on us. Dave, put some guys on it, try to find out what the Penetrator is up to. Meanwhile, gentlemen, we've got to go on as though nothing matters. What's this other problem, Randy?"

"Jesse Deerhorn still refuses to sell. He threatened to have my man arrested for trespass this morning."

"Damn that thick-headed Indian. Doesn't he have any better sense than that? We need that place for an access road to the new coal vein behind here."

"He don't give a reason, Johnny, he just tells us hell no. And he's still displaying campaign posters for Nelson Lemmon. We've torn down half a dozen, he keeps on putting them up. This last one he has boobytrapped with a stick of dynamite. My boys are afraid to touch it."

"Goddamn that stupid redskin! He's gotta be taught a lesson. Randy, I want you meet with some of your boys. Figure out a way to handle Deerhorn. I don't want any more Lemmon posters on his land and I want him to sell before the end of this week. See to it." He turned to Dave Guthrie.

"Dave, get on the phone to your office in Birmingham. Tell someone there to pass the word to the street people and your own informants. Say there'll be a thousand dollar reward to anyone who turns in this Penetrator guy."

Chapter 6
Bloody Politics

For purposes of security, the former Piggly-Wiggly supermarket, with its gaudily bedecked windows, had been shunned for this meeting. No one wanted the possibility of a chance overhearing of the discussion.

Instead they chose Johnny Herter's business office, where the conduct of his various legitimate enterprises was regulated from the high-rise Union Bank building on Commerce Street. Those present had a spectacular view from the large windows of the southwest corner room, overlooking the Civic Center complex, Old Union Depot, and Riverside Park. Sightseeing, however, was far from being the purpose of the session.

"Johnny, I'm sure you're acquainted with Leroy Tuttle and Moses Sims. And, at least by reputation, you know Beau Cranston from the Democratic Central Committee." Dave Guthrie made the introductions smoothly, almost unctuously.

"Oh, yeah. I've known these boys a long time. How are you, Moses, Leroy? Mr. Cranston and I've talked on the phone before. Nice to be meeting you in person. Now, let's get down to basics. What are you people prepared to do for me?"

Cranston looked uncomfortable, as though embarrassed by Herter's lack of tact and diplomacy. He believed politics should be a gentlemanly avocation, dispassionately debated, decisions genially rendered. Johnny Herter came on far too strong for his liking. He opened his mouth to make a moderating statement, but Johnny plunged on.

"Look, we all know the score. Otherwise you wouldn't be here, right? I'm the only hope you've got to rally the black vote and the liberal vote behind the Democratic banner. Look. I'm sorry . . . and I'm deeply disturbed by what happened to Andy Wells. He was a friend. We go back a long ways. The fact remains that you decided, behind the scenes, to dump your own man, Nelson Lemmon, in favor of Andy. You needed Wells because he represented the trend developing in your party on the national level. I do too. So, we simply can't sit on our butts mourning Andy and watch this election go down the tubes as well. After the primary, with the right candidate, you can beat anyone the Republicans come up with. I'm right on that, ain't I?"

"You certainly are, Johnny. I . . . we . . . all of us who backed Andy . . . ah, well, we know you're the only one who supports the high-minded goals he had. You are the only candidate who would carry out some of the reforms and other projects he wanted to bring into being."

"Moses is right, Johnny. The entire black population of Alabama will back you."

"Thank you, Leroy. I appreciate that. But then, why shouldn't they back me? I'm their great white hope, right?" Johnny broke up in giggling laughter at his crude and tasteless pun. Dave Guthrie came to the sudden realization that Johnny had somehow managed to snort more than one paper of coke. He could only hope Herter wouldn't turn vicious and bloodthirsty.

"I feel that was entirely uncalled for," Beau Cranston said coldly.

Herter sobered. He needed Cranston to tip the balance in his direction. "Forgive me, boys. I sometimes have a flash of gutter humor. It's a leftover from my days as a lumberjack. I'm sorry. No one admired Andy Wells more than me. And, as you know, I've always been in the forefront of the civil rights movement. That's where I met Andy. Don't know what come over me to say a thing like that. No offense?"

"A magnanimous apology, Mr. Herter. I feel that I'm gaining some insight into the greatness others attribute to you through this. Further, it certainly justifies the decision the Central Committee made, which I'm to present to you tonight. As chairman of that committee, it is my duty to inform you that by unanimous vote, you have been selected as the draft replacement for Andy Wells to run against Nelson Lemmon. Bear in mind, Nelson will still be receiving support. He is, after all, the incumbent. But we feel that the party can best serve the people by giving them an opportunity to make a clear choice between differing viewpoints. It was felt that of all the possible replacements, you most fully represent the principles for which Andy stood."

Herter's face took on a look of feigned astonishment mixed with pleasure. He was a consummate actor; even the drugs ravaging his brain failed to interfere with his well-rehearsed performance. "I'm overwhelmed, Mr. Cranston. Really I am. Oh, I sat in on several discussions with members of your committee, but I hardly thought they'd be that serious in considering me. I changed my voter registration when APP was formed. Now I suppose I'll have to come back to the fold. Thank you . . . thank you all. I . . . I shall do everything I can to repay your trust"

"I'm certain you will. We won't go into details now. Your staff will be integrated with the regular party machinery over the next two days and we can iron out any rough edges then. Now, I think we should go."

"Thank you again, gentlemen, all of you," Herter said while Dave Guthrie saw the visitors to the door.

From the entrance to an adjoining office, Porter Carson wheeled himself into the room, followed by several of Herter's top aides. When the hall door closed behind the departing delegation, Herter turned to his cohorts and released a high-pitched but restrained rebel yell.

"We got 'em where we want 'em, boys. How about that? It's official now, drafted as candidate for the party. You see, Porter? I told you we didn't have to worry about any repercussions over hitting Wells. Nothing came of it. Nothing but good, that is."

"So far you seem to be accurate on that, Johnny. Thank goodness we have only the one killing to worry about."

"Uh, don't be so sure of that, Porter. Boys, I think the time is right for us to line up Belman to make a hit on my only opposition, Nelson Lemmon."

Porter Carson paled. "You can't be serious, Johnny."

"I've never been more convinced of the importance of something."

"It's insane," a young, long-haired man wearing

64

rimless granny glasses burst into the conversation. "The people would never stand for it. Why . . . why it goes against everything, all reason. People want to think they have a choice, even if it's between two sides of the same coin. They'd make such a noise about it that it would get everyone in on it— our state agencies, the feds, everyone."

"To hell with the people!" Filled with the savage and irresolute humor brought about by his body's unusual reaction to cocaine, Johnny Herter burned with fury. "And to hell with them having any say in things. The best choice for the people at election time is *no choice at all*. That's been proven over and over. People need someone to make their decisions for them . . . in advance. Keeps 'em from being confused.

"Hell, even them limp-wristed, Ivy League types up North know that. You ever hear Teddy make a speech that didn't have an implied assurance that he knew more about what people needed and how they should live their lives than they did? Jesus, here you guys are, callin' yourselves liberals an' activists an' revisionists, and you don't even know what all that intellectual shit is about. The fact that half of you are in this for the graft you can get and only those remaining are motivitated by political idealism doesn't alter the basic reality. The so-called activists of today, no matter what sugar coating they wrap their programs in, are as anxious to institute absolute authority and control over every aspect of every person's life as any fascist dictator of the past. I knew that long before I got into politics. Power is the name of the game. Getting that power takes a lot of balls. So don't go giving me all this crap about whether we should or should not eliminate the competition. I say we pass the word to Belman that he's to hit Nelson Lemmon."

Ed Merril, wearing a Union Bank janitor's uniform, leaned against the wall outside Johnny Herter's office. The needle on the VU meter of his tape recorder jerked erratically, indicating that the contact mike attached to the door recorded faithfully the conversation within. What he had managed to overhear so far, through the small earplug attachment, left him astounded. He couldn't possibly believe that Johnny Herter was serious in what he'd discussed with his associates. Admitting to arranging the murder of one candidate for the opportunity to be placed in the position of being the party's replacement was bad enough. The cold-blooded decision to kill the only other opponent went beyond sanity. The whole thing constituted journalistic dynamite.

He'd do it up in two parts for *Floodlight*, send them off at the same time, then take the tape and his own observations to the state elections board and the attorney general. Ed's mind raced as he strained to hear more from beyond the office door. The sudden sound of a motor activating one of the building's elevators brought him away from his listening post. He quickly detached the contact mike and shoved the recorder into a plastic bag-lined metal trash can. He grabbed a mop and pail from the custodial cart and moved away from Herter's office. He was whistling softly and contentedly swabbing the hallway floor when the car stopped on that floor and a man got out of the elevator.

The newcomer gave Ed Merril only a passing mildly curious glance as he walked down the hall.

Stopping before Herter's office, he knocked, then let himself in.

"Hey, am I seeing things?" Larry Flowers asked those assembled inside Herter's office.

"Like what, Larry?"

"There's a janitor on this floor and he . . ."

"I thought you instructed the head custodian to keep his people off this floor until we left, Dave," Herter snapped, interrupting his aide.

"I did."

"Well, there's one out there now," Flowers defended his earlier statement. "And I'll swear he looks exactly like that damned *Floodlight* reporter, Ed Merril."

"Sonofabitch!" Herter exploded. He turned to the longhair, who stood polishing his granny glasses. "Sammy, get on the phone to Belman. Tell him he has two hits coming. That's right. You, Larry and Mike, go check out the hall. If that is Merril, we'll have to fix his clock."

Chapter 7
Carbon-Copy Clue

All through the night, Ed Merril worked on his compromise solution. He completed the two *Floodlight* articles and put them in a separate envelopes. This was too hot to leave at home. He'd take them along and put the copies in his safe deposit box. He did additional work for the local newspapers, including copies of his photos of the orgy, and hinted heavily of a big revelation to come soon. The attorney general would want to hear the tape, so he removed it from the recorder and dropped it in a side jacket pocket. He felt heavy with fatigue but shunned sleep in order to get this task completed. By late the next morning, he had everything in readiness.

Ed picked up the large manila envelope containing his stories and photos and kissed his wife. Climbing behind the wheel of his Honda CVCC, he fired up the engine and headed down the long mountain grade from his home, driving toward Gadsden, the nearest town. The Honda's small engine purred quietly and, with the windows down, Ed enjoyed the trip. Drawing in deep draughts of crisp air, he felt himself rejuvenating from his long ordeal at the typewriter and enlarger. Peripherally he noticed a looming bulk behind him. Checking his rearview mirror, Ed saw a huge tractor-trailer drawing closer to his rear bumper, the gigantic diesel engine bellowing lustily.

"What the hell!" Ed spoke aloud his thoughts. "Did that guy lose his brakes?" Ed jinked to the side to allow more room.

The truck, as quickly as possible to respond to Ed's movement, swerved over to once more line up behind. Worried now, Ed Merril gave the Honda more gas. A series of sharp curves appeared ahead. One way or another he would shake the pursuing eighteen wheeler there. A rig like that simply couldn't make the turns as fast as he could. Ed increased his spced slightly, drawing away from the truck.

As Ed slammed into the first curve, he momentarily lost sight of the big Peterbuilt cab. Taking the best line, which evened out the bend by running from one side to the other, he prayed no one would be coming up the grade. The light CVCC had a tendency to fishtail at high speeds in turns, so Ed carefully countersteered as he felt the back end let go. Down into the second twist he lost evcn the roaring sound of the throaty diesel. His palms began to sweat, but now he relaxed his hands on the wheel. As he came out of the final sweep, he checked his rearview mirror and saw nothing behind. He looked back at the road and slowed slightly. Suddenly the bull-throated bellow from twin chrome stacks shattered his confidence.

This was no runaway. The trucker had geared down to negotiate the curves safely, then had come roaring after him. Whoever sat behind the wheel of the big rig was out to kill him, Ed realized with chilling preception. Shoving his foot to the floorboard, he urged every last mile of speed from the little import car.

Sweat beaded Ed's forehead and his face paled with fear as he glanced into the mirror, watching the eighteen wheeler draw inexorably closer. Had he not been holding the steering wheel, Ed's hands would have trembled uncontrollably. His mind raced silently, clamoring at the car to produce more speed. He'd make it, *he had to make it!* he thought frantically. A quick glance, to reassure himself he was holding his own, robbed him of control of his sphincter muscles.

A large wet spot spread from Ed's crotch as he watched the field of the rearview mirror fill with high chrome bumper and the squarish, brutal-looking rectangle of the truck's radiator. In a frantic effort he tried swerving. The Peterbuilt hung on tenaciously. Ed jerked the wheel in the opposite direction as he thought in total panic, *Mother of God, he's going to kill me!*

"Hail Holy Queen, Mother of Mercy, our life, our sweetness, our hope . . ." Ed prayed aloud as his ears vibrated with the pounding sound of diesel cylinders and blatting exhaust. Only inches separated the two vehicles as Ed hoped frantically to make the next series of curves, something to slow down the menacing truck, or for a highway patrolman to suddenly appear, or to awaken to find himself in bed beside his lovely wife, shaken by a nightmare, but safe.

Oh, my God—Ann. What would she do? Three kids to take care of and her pregnant with the fourth. *"Dear God, don't let me die!"* Ed's mind shrieked, his terror making him say the words

71

aloud. All light blanked out of the rear window as the truck closed even more.

A tentative thump that quickly withdrew brought a throat-scarring shriek of terror from Ed's lips, the last sound he would ever make on this earth. The shrill scream of horror continued as the truck slammed into the rear of Ed's Honda, shoving it toward the edge of the road, just short of the next curve. The CVCC's tires *yowled* and smoked in protest as the gigantic mass of the Peterbuilt crumpled metal, snapped the drive shaft, and drove Ed Merril to the guard rail. The tough, corrugated strip gave under the weight and shock of impact and Ed's Honda hurtled out into space above a dropoff of some three hundred feet.

Braking adroitly, Art Belman barely managed to avoid following Ed Merril to his death below. The Peterbuilt snorted into reverse and regained the road while the sounds of impact and end-over-end, rolling disintegration came from below. Giving a light hearted "Shave and a Haircut" toot to the tractor's air horns, Belman began to grind upward through the gears.

"An unexplained and unwitnessed accident late this morning claimed the life of investigative reporter Ed Merril of rural Gadsden. The accident occurred on a mountainous stretch of County Road 71, several miles from Merril's home. Fire destroyed the automobile and its contents and forestry units were required to contain the blaze. Mr. Merril, who was known to millions of readers across the nation for his startling exposé articles in the pages of *Floodlight* . . ." Johnny Herter snapped off the radio.

He expressed his satisfaction through a spreading grin.

"Hot damn. Belman came through for us. We won't have to worry about that nosey damn reporter any more."

"I'm not so sure of that. Killing a politician, and a black one at that, was dangerous enough. Now you've had a member of the press hit. I think things are getting out of hand, Johnny." Porter Carson rolled his wheelchair away from the desk, his features betraying his anxiety. He stared out the large picture windows to the distant Alabama River and the placid activity of the riverboat, General Richard Montgomery.

"Still worried about my idea of hitting Nelson Lemmon, Porter? No need to. Hell, who could ever connect it up to us?"

"The Penetrator could."

"Forget him. Nothing's surfaced on the guy since his try for Belman. My money says he's working on the Syndicate thing in Atlanta. It's likely we'll never hear from him again."

"I wouldn't put more than a five dollar bill on that, if I were you, Johnny."

"Mrs. Merril?" the Penetrator asked in subdued, sympathetic tones. "We're sorry to call on you at such a time. It is important, though. We're looking into anything that might have even a remote connection to the assassination of Andrew Wells." Mark showed the grieving widow his false Justice Department ID.

"I'm afraid this may be a bit upsetting," Samantha Chase added gently. "We'll try to be brief."

"Won't you please come in?" Ann Merril asked, showing them into a brightly lighted living room that overlooked the shelving hills in a spectacular view of pine forest. She stood only a bit over five-three, barefoot, wearing a loose housedress that roundly bulged with advanced pregnancy. Her eyes, red and puffed from weeping, were a startlingly clear blue, emphasized by long dark lashes and arched, full brows. She indicated a couch, then seated herself on a chair opposite.

At Mark's nod, Sam took the lead. "We'll try not to make this too unpleasant. No doubt the highway patrol has already told you this. Their report indicates that another vehicle, a semi-trailer truck, might have been involved in the . . . ah, accident that took your husband's life. Do you know of anyone who might want to see him killed?"

"Murder you mean?" Ann Merril thought a moment. "Oh, there are a couple of union bosses, some minor organized crime figures. But surely . . . I mean, Ed is . . . uh, *was* primarily a political writer."

"Did that include Andy Wells?" Mark asked next.

"No. Not really. Ed didn't like what Wells stood for, naturally, but his main interest was in Johnny Herter. Ed called him corrupt and ambitious. He believed Herter entered politics only to obtain a power base from which he could dispense favors and enrich himself in the process. Ed was preparing a series on Herter. He worked all last night on it. Now . . . now he's . . . dead." Tears welled in her eyes as she realized the finality of the words she had spoken. Silence held for a long while.

Shrill children's voices, raised in argument,

came from the rear of the house. Ann surmounted her grief, becoming the complete mother. "Jimmy, Brian. Y'all stop that, ya hear?"

A barefoot tow-head about nine years of age appeared suddenly in the doorway. He was clad in cut-offs and a T-shirt. "Aaawh, M-o-m!"

"Don't give me that, young man. You children go outside and play. Y'all got no reason to be . . . moping . . . around . . . the house." She choked back a sob as the boy disappeared down the hallway, calling to his siblings.

"C'mon Brian, Cissy, let's go down to the pond. Mom's got vis-a-tors."

"Please excuse me." Ann Merril mopped at overflowing eyes. "This has all come at . . . such an inopportune time." Hearing herself and examining the words, she burst into brittle laughter, tinged with a bit of hysteria. "Oh, God, what am I saying? Forgive me, please?"

The Penetrator picked up the conversation at the point before their interruption. "You say he was working on the Herter articles last night? Is it possible he developed any connection between Herter and Wells?"

"Not that I know of. Outside of their political pronouncements being a little left of Fidel Castro, they had hardly anything in common. Wells came from a poor black family in Montgomery, Herter is a millionaire several times over. Ed was excited about something he uncovered last night, though. He worked on it all through until this morning. He was on his way to mail the manuscript when . . . when he went off the road. Would you like to see what he was working on?"

"Certainly. Did he leave a copy?"

"He always made carbons for his files. Come with me. Ed's office is upstairs."

Half an hour later, Mark and Sam had gone through Ed Merril's file on Johnny Herter. Although there was nothing showing a solid connection between Herter, Wells, and the death of the reporter, a strong hunch began to grow in the Penetrator's mind. He riffled back through the pages of manuscript of the newspaper articles, willing them to say what he wanted them to say. " 'A startling revelation is about to break in the checkered career of rags-to-riches candidate Johnny Herter.' But what revelation? If it referred to the killing of Wells, why didn't Merril come out and say so? 'Sinister plans of Herter's campaign staff are only a part of the bloody contest for the Alabama senatorial seat of Nelson Lemmon.' What sinister plans, Sam?" A subhead caught Mark's attention: WILL YET ANOTHER CANDIDATE DIE? "Lots of loaded innuendo surrounding far too few facts. Damnit, this all has to connect up somewhere, despite Merril's florid writing style."

"Look at this." Samatha Chase, who had been examining the rest of Merril's private files, came to where Mark stood trying to make the mute typed words scream an accusation. "Profiles on all of Herter's campaign staff. Here's a real sweetheart. Dave Guthrie. He's a big money man from Birmingham. Guthrie handles the campaign finances. Seems he's also a fixer, a grease man who uses his connections and a little long green to cover up the peccadillos of the big shots. He's also into a thing called God's Blood, whatever that is. And he represents some small coal companies as a fund raiser."

"Marvelous. Where does that take us in regard to

Wells' murder?" The fingers of Mark's right hand toyed idly with Merril's tape recorder. He released the catch for the cassette compartment. It was empty. As he lifted the leather carrying case, he noticed a slip of paper shoved between it and the metal body of the machine. He pulled it out, glanced at it and handed it to Sam.

Samantha read aloud. " 'Another murder is planned.' Okay, but who is the victim, Stan? Merril, himself? Herter? Nelson Lemmon? The Republican opposition? We don't have the answers. I think we'd better pay a call on some people."

"Right. Beginning with Dave Guthrie."

Chapter 8
Never Argue with a Lady

The Penetrator had a hard time talking Sam Chase out of it, but he managed to make his visit to Dave Guthrie's office alone, while she ran down more information on Herter, Guthrie, and God's Blood. To some extent, Mark considered this foray into Guthrie's activities a blind shot at best. Nothing they'd seen connected Guthrie or Herter with Wells. He decided, however, to give it all he could.

"Good morning, may I help you?" a streamlined blonde-by-request asked the Penetrator when he entered the tastefully expensive reception area.

"Yes. I'm Stan McDade. I'd like to see Mr. Guthrie regarding a contribution to the Herter campaign."

"You could do that through his regular campaign office, Mr. McDade."

"Not in the figures I'm thinking of."

"I see. Just a moment, please." The taut-bodied secretary rose and crossed to tall oak double-doors that gave access to an inner office. She went in, closing the portal behind her. In a few moments she returned, wearing a less cordial smile.

"It seems no one is familiar with your name, Mr., ah, McDade. If you could give me a better idea of what you have in mind . . ."

The Penetrator checked the nameplate on her desk. "Well, Miss Larson, I'm not prepared to discuss this with anyone but Mr. Guthrie. Would you please tell him I'm here?"

"It's *Ms.* Larson, if you don't mind. Mr. Guthrie is out of the office this morning. In any case, it would be Mr. Tate you'd be seeing. He's the one actually handling the Herter funds."

"Then I'll see him *now*."

"Really, Mr. McDade, we aren't accustomed to conducting our business in this unorthodox manner."

Mark tried a smile. It failed to warm Larson's icy eyes. "Then unbend a little for once and be a bit unorthodox. We're talking about a great deal of money, Ms. Larson. The sum I have in mind can't be discussed under the watchful eye of the Federal Elections Commission."

"Mr. McDade, I must insist you be more specific."

"And I insist on seeing your Mr. Tate. He's the only one I'll give the details to."

Relenting, but still resentful of the challenge to her authority, Dorothy Larson keyed her intercom, spoke a few words. "He'll see you, though I don't understand why. Turn to your left and it's the second door on the right."

Cy Tate turned out to be a toad of a man—round of face, neckless, with sloping shoulders atop a rotund body built close to the ground. His protuberant eyes, small, sleeked-back ears, and wide mouth added to the image. He spoke with the airy gasps of a chronic asthmatic.

"Ah, Mr. McDade. You're a persistent man to get past Dorothy out there. Take a seat and tell me what you came here for." He extended a hand that was dry and cold, completing the toad-like image.

"Mr. Tate, I represent a . . . ah, consortium of businessmen who wish to lend support to Johnny Herter's campaign. Actually, I came to see Dave Guthrie about it."

"Dave's out of the office. I'm sure Dorothy told you that. Perhaps I can handle the matter. Precisely what sort of support do you intend to provide?"

"We were thinking in terms of twenty-five thousand dollars."

Tate's thin eyebrows rose toward his receding hairline. "Oooh. I see. I'm sure you realize that federal election statutes limit such donations to two hundred and fifty dollars at any one time."

"That's why I'm here. We have a fat bundle of cash and we don't want to dribble it out over a long period."

"Naturally you would expect the new senator to be properly grateful for this largess?"

"There would be more, of course, after the primary."

"To what end?"

"The men I represent are in the contracting and building business. In particular, bridges, highways, dams . . . that sort of thing. Senators are in a position to exercise their influence on matters inside the state, say as to whom a contract is given. They also have a certain power as to where and how federal money is spent."

"Hmmm. A most interesting theory. Perhaps a newly elected senator wouldn't be as able as you think."

"We're willing to take that gamble . . . if the right considerations are made."

"That's something I can't speak for the senator on, but it will be brought to his attention. Where can we reach you?"

"My principals wish this to remain an anonymous gift. I'll contact you tomorrow afternoon. Will that be enough time?"

"I'm sure it will."

"Thank you."

The Penetrator left Guthrie's office with his hunch node humming away like a vibrator. He'd learned one important thing. Johnny Herter could be bought. Now the question arose if Herter was an honest politician—one who stayed bought. It also remained to be seen if Herter's venality sat at the center of his ambition or indicated only a symptom of greater corruption. Something like using assassination to gain political office.

After the Penetrator left, Dave Guthrie entered Cy Tate's office. He came from his own lavish appointments behind the large double doors. "We got him on tape, Cy. You buy his story?"

Cy Tate lowered lazy lids over his pop-eyes. A pink ribbon of tongue flicked over thin lips. "Could be. We haven't heard from the contractors as yet. This might be their man."

"Whichever way it goes down, I think we'd better call Johnny." He reached over to Tate's phone and punched out a number.

"Thanks for filling me in, Dave," Johnny Herter told his finance man after Guthrie had described Mark's visit. "The way I see it, we have two routes to go. First, if he is genuine, you find out exactly how much the contractors will shake down for. I figure them for at least a million. Hell, they make that several times over on a single highway contract. The way things are, they should be happy to cough up five times that, but they're too cheap. I'll settle for a round figure of a cool mill. Now, on the second course . . ."

"That's what I've been thinking about, Johnny. From what I saw of this guy on the TV monitor, he matches the description Belman's keepers gave us of the Penetrator."

A long pause followed. "That occurred to me, too, Dave. I think I'd better send a team up there to look into things. They should be there in an hour and a half, two at the most. So hang tight and let's see what they turn up."

"You *have* had a busy day, Sam," Mark told Samantha Chase when they met at their motel later in the day. He eyed the closely written script on the ruled, yellow legal pad she held on her lap.

"Thank you, kind sir, but any rookie detective could have accomplished the same thing, just as safely. Did you know that Guthrie is business manager of God's Blood?"

"No. What's that got to do with it?"

"That's the band that Johnny Herter thinks is the heavenly choir. Three of their members are, as of yesterday, under indictment by a federal grand jury for conspiracy to transport illegal narcotics interstate for the purpose of sale, possession of narcotics for sale, conspiracy to commit murder, and the murder of a federal narcotics officer. Thanks to high-level, but unnamed, intervention, they are all out on bail. And, to date, their case has not even been put on the trial calendar."

Mark whistled softly. "With Herter and our boy

Guthrie up to their ears in the activities of this band of Boy Scouts, it puts an interesting light on things. Add that to their apparent cautious willingness to accept a bribe and Herter comes off looking a bit dirtier than what shows on the surface. What else did you get?"

"Herter and Guthrie both hold a financial interest in Paragon Security." To Mark's surprised, "Hmmm," she went on. "That's what I thought. The same outfit that provided bodyguards for Art Belman. It looks to me like there's a definite connection between Herter and the killing of Andy Wells."

"Exactly. But we don't have what we need to prove it."

"Damnit, McDade, what else is there to get?"

"Evidence. Hard facts that will stand up in court. Or, if we fail to get that, an absolute conviction that Herter is responsible and had ought to be taken off."

"Jesus, you're hard. You mean, *pow!*, just like that you'd blow him away?"

"If I couldn't develop any other way of stopping him, yes. Working only from the outside won't provide enough information for either course. That means getting into Herter's operation."

"Okay. When do I start?"

"Whoa. Hold it. This thing can get dangerous, Sam. If Herter is involved in the assassination of Wells, you can be sure he wouldn't hesitate a moment about killing someone caught snooping inside his organization. The fact you're female wouldn't buy you anything. I'm sure, too, that I've had a lot more experience infiltrating setups like this than you have."

"In this instance, that doesn't matter. I have a distinct advantage over you. I look, or can do myself up to look the part. You can't."

"Don't argue, Sam. I won't let you try it."

"You won't *let* me? Look, you might be damn good, the best, maybe, but I have a special weapon when it comes to wangling information on the sly."

"Spell that out for me."

"You said it yourself. Because I am female. You may have your mother's features, but you've got your father's fixtures. That gives me an enormous advantage over you when it comes to finding the weak link in Herter's chain of command and getting him to spill what he knows."

The Penetrator blinked, as though he didn't quite believe what he'd heard. Then a small smile began to quirk the corners of his mouth. In a second they were laughing together, the tension easing.

"Oh, Sam, Sam. You've made your point. Red Eagle always says never to argue with a woman. That they know where all the skeletons lay buried and can twist your words tighter than a bullsnake can squeeze a rat."

"Who is Red Eagle?"

"Never mind. All right, you win on this, temporarily at least. Go ahead and infiltrate Herter's campaign staff if you can. But promise me this. At the first hint of the least little suspicion on their part, you split out of there and get to a safe place. You understand me? Now, I'm going to go get a look at Paragon Security. When I come back we're going to make mad, ferocious love, eat a big steak, and head for Montgomery."

The Penetrator wasn't aware of the pair of small, nondescript cars that set up a leap-frog tail on him

85

as he left the motel. He had them made, though, long before he reached Paragon Security. When he pulled to the curb outside the building that housed the offices of the private police force, four men scrambled from the lead vehicle. Scattering the few pedestrians on the sidewalk, they made a dash toward Mark, two swinging blackjacks and the others reaching under their coats for weapons.

Chapter 9
Injun Trouble

The Penetrator quickly took the *T-Dachi* triangle-defense stance, facing so all four men were in his range of vision. This karate position, identical to one basic position in the Native American martial art of *Orenda Keowa*, allows the practitioner to move quickly and lethally from defense to offense. As the attackers closed, Mark kept his eyes moving, so that each man remained in view.

"Hey, Lem, it's one of them karate freaks. This is gonna be fun." His next remarks were aimed at the Penetrator. "Hey, sucker, that fancy sport shit ain't gonna help you a . . . *yiiiii!*" His brag broke off into a painful yelp as the Penetrator's leading foot snapped forward and up, the toe of his shoe connecting with the blackjack-wielding thug's kneecap, dislocating it from its socket.

Mark reversed directions, delivering a back kick that caused Lem to leap away. "Web! Shoot him for Christ's sake," Lem shouted.

Webster Blount found his gun arm being lifted out and away from his body, then descending while the man they came to rough up pivoted and brought his leg surging upward. A dry-stick snapping preceded Web's shriek of agony when the Penetrator broke his arm. The .38 Special fell from his useless fingers. Mark shoved the now-whimpering gunman into the fourth member of the team.

Hobbling painfully, their leader rejoined the fight, launching himself bodily at the Penetrator. Mark knelt quickly, taking the flying body by one arm and the seat of the pants. Trouser cloth tore as he hurled the man into the welter of arms and legs of the other two. The Penetrator sprang to his feet and gave Lem a *Shuto* blow to the soft paunch that overhung his belt. Gasping and choking, Lem staggered away to retch into the gutter.

Norman Hart, the fourth member of Herter's goon squad, managed to pull himself clear of Web Blount and Fred Hubbard long enough to draw his .380 Savage auto and snap off a shot at the Penetrator. The small slug missed, pockmarking the cement wall beyond where Mark stood. Then Norman found himself looking into the wide, black hole at the muzzle of the Penetrator's Star PD. Red-orange flame bloomed and expanded toward him, nearly as fast as the .45-jacketed hollow point that bit into his flesh below the right collar bone and expended its energy, smashing a ragged hole through Norman's shoulder blade.

Lem turned back at the sound of the two shots. He rushed to where the others sprawled on the sidewalk. "For Christ's sake, let's get out of here, Fred," he yelled at their leader.

Fred proved his leadership ability, acting with alacrity under the commanding bulk of the .45 auto in the Penetrator's hand. He and Lem helped their injured partners into the car and sped away. The occupants of the other vehicle had fled with screeching tires at the sound of the first shot. Behind them, the Penetrator calmly reholstered his Star PD and bent to pick up the wallet that had fallen from Fred's torn trouser pocket.

"Interesting. It's a piece of that solid evidence we wanted, but what does it point to?" the Penetrator speculated aloud as he read a card in the wallet that identified Fred Golinsky as an employee of Paragon Security and another that stated he was a member of the security force for the Johnny Herter for Senate Campaign Committee. He'd tell Sam about it later at the motel. Provided she managed to get inside Herter's organization, he'd have her look into it. The thought suddenly occurred to him that with Herter's men coming into the open like this, the danger to Sam would be greatly increased. He didn't like that at all.

"What do you mean he shot you the hell up, kicked the shit out of you, and got away without a scratch?" Johnny Herter thundered at a chastened and embarrassed Fred Golinsky that evening in Herter's Montgomery campaign headquarters.

"I'm sorry, boss. I mean it. Hell, this guys's a pro. He had us on our asses before we knew what was happening. Norman tried to put a slug in him and damn near got blown away for it. Jeez, I've never seen a man move so fast. I always thought that karate stuff was a lot of crap. The doc says I'll have to walk with a cane for the next six months."

"You four were supposed to be the best on the payroll. What a hell of a screwup. Well, if you can't handle a pro, maybe you can take care of a couple of dumb Indians. Jesse Deerhorn's still being stubborn. I want you to pick up some more of the boys and go up to Calhoun County and convince him to change his mind."

Fred Golinsky turned to leave but stopped at the sound of Johnny's voice. "You're a lucky man, Fred. You know that?"

"How's that, boss?"

"You're one of a few people who've met the Penetrator and lived to talk about it."

It's not right, Steve Deerhorn thought. His father, Jesse, had a reputation as a man who didn't push easily. Unfortunately, his stubbornness lacked any positive action. *Rather than do something to bring an end to the harassment by that Left-wing creep, Herter, Dad just stands there saying, 'I won't sell,'* Steve's thoughts went on. The younger Deerhorn was a veteran of Viet Nam, proud of his Chickasaw Indian ancestry, impatient and frustrated by what he saw around him.

That morning, before Steve left to sell hogs in Gadsden, Jesse had told him of Herter's latest offer. Their discussion turned into a brief argument. "Jesus Christ, Dad!" Steve snapped, letting his anger spill over. "Talk about the corruption in the Saigon government. Well, I was there and I saw it and I'll tell you this: People ought to take a good look around. They should see what's going on right here. Herter and his gang make the Diem government look like a bunch of Boy Scouts."

Steve had left then, grinding through the gears while the truck's exhaust snorted out his anger. He hadn't traveled half a mile before he began to regret the choleric scene with his father. Arguing with an elder showed disrespect and that was not the Indian way.

Once he'd sold the hogs and collected the check, Steve started home, his mind still dwelling on the situation. His thirst got the better of him, though, when he spotted the MILLERS sign down the road a ways. He might as well hit the Rebel Yell for a couple of brews. It might take his mind off their troubles, Steve decided. He eased the truck into the parking lot and climbed from the cab.

Half an hour later, Steve finished his second beer and started for the door. He never saw who threw the first punch. A hard-knuckled fist caught him in the side of the head. Stunned, Steve stumbled against the wall. Then four men were on him, punching, stomping, and kicking. He bit back a cry of pain as he felt a rib break, tried to cover his face and blacked out as a cowboy boot slammed into his temple.

Sam Chase stood at a tall metal filing cabinet, placing letters in alphabetized folders. She looked up as five men, one of them limping badly and using a cane, entered the Montgomery campaign headquarters. Their gleeful laughter and harsh voices seemed to fill the former supermarket.

"It's a good thing that Calhoun chief deputy is on our payroll, huh boys? Did you hear what he said after we pulled you guys off that Deerhorn punk?" Fred Golinsky, the limping one, said to the others. Screwing up his features into a disapproving look, he mimicked the stern tones of the Herter-bribed sheriff. " 'Now you boys shouldn't oughta take your politics so seriously. Even if this Injun punk called Mr. Herter a sonofabitch, that's no call to mess him up so bad. Personally I think Mr. Herter's gonna make a fine senator, but a beer hall's no place to argue politics.' An' then he let us go."

"Whoo boy! Fred, I gotta hand it to you. If that don't make those no-good trash sell to Johnny, nothin' will."

They passed by Sam with only a few appraising looks at her well-turned legs and protruding chest. The clatter of a bottle neck against a glass rim and rattle of ice cubes coming from the staff lounge indicated they would be occupied for some time. Sam finished her assigned task and left the building.

As Sam drove north out of Montgomery on US 231, she wondered what she'd find in Gadsden. After her phone conversation with the Penetrator that morning, she had no difficulty recognizing Fred Golinsky as one of the security men who had jumped him outside the Paragon offices. Now Golinsky and the others came back from a trip to Calhoun County joking about stomping someone, an Indian she gathered, into the ground. She and the Penetrator were both interested in anything regarding Herter so she decided to make a quick trip north to find out what bearing, if any, this had on the case they were trying to make.

Three hours later, Sam had a story that could have come right out of Western fiction. Seated next to Steve Deerhorn's bed in the Gadsden hospital, she had listened as he and his father, Jesse, told of Herter's activities attempting to force them to sell their small farm. It butted against Herter's Pine Grove plantation and from the time Herter had arrived in the area, he'd been after Jesse to sell. Lately his efforts had increased. To Sam it came on like the old frontier cliché of the greedy land baron scheming to force out the squatters. Once she had all the details, Sam called the motel in Birmingham.

When she finished filling Mark in on the beating of Steve Deerhorn and Fred Golinsky's comments, there was a long silence. At last Mark spoke. "Okay, Sam. I think we have enough now to take it to the authorities. I'll go to the attorney general's office in Montgomery tomorrow."

Chapter 10
Legal Snare

Having given in once to Sam's schemes, the Penetrator was determined not to do so again. He firmly refuted her reasons for wanting to meet him at the state building, convincing her at last to stay out of that end of the case. She should, he informed her, dig deeper into Herter's activities. "Keep after him, but keep out of trouble," he had admonished. Consequently, he arrived at the attorney general's office alone.

"Good morning, sir. May I help you?"

Mark wondered if secretaries to bureaucrats were manufactured somewhere on an assembly line and issued out by a supply sergeant. All those he'd ever had occasion to deal with seemed uniformly polite, moderately attractive, exuding an air of competent efficiency. He explained, without actually revealing anything, his purpose in being there to this one, whom he mentally labeled as Secretary, Judicial Branch, State Level, General Purpose.

"You'd want to talk with one of the deputy attorneys, then. One moment, please." She keyed the intercom and spoke into it briefly, then turned back to Mark. "Right down the inner hallway, there. Room 304. Mr. Bolt will be handling your case."

"Come in," a voice called in response to Mark's knock. The Penetrator entered Room 304 to find a man standing behind a cluttered desk, hand extended and a smile in place. Bolt's physique clearly showed the ravages of a sedentary life on an once-athletic body. "I'm Jim Bolt. I'll be going over this with you to determine what kind of case, if any, we have. Sit down, Mr. . . . ?

"McDade. Stan McDade, Mr. Bolt."

"Good." Bolt, whose grip had been firm, withdrew his hand from Mark's and returned to his chair. "Now, let's hear what you have."

Jim Bolt frowned, nodded, and made short notes on a long, yellow legal pad while the Penetrator described to him the evidence he and Sam had obtained. When Mark concluded, Bolt sat staring darkly at the paper before him, lips pursed, a frown creasing his forehead. Like all successful attorneys, Jim Bolt was a consummate actor. He did not betray by any gesture, word, or facial expression that his name was on Johnny Herter's secret list of bought officials. He broke his feigned study when he decided the tension had sufficiently built.

"This is an extremely serious accusation you've made, Mr. McDade. Oh, you seem to have developed plenty of information. If the evidence proves out to be as you've indicated, there's ample grounds to initiate an investigation by this office, toward the end of presenting it to a grand jury. But with the primary only four days away, this merits somewhat more expeditious handling. Let me take it directly to the attorney general. Would you mind waiting in the outer office?"

Mark excused himself and returned to the reception area. He selected a squarish, uncomfortable-appearing chair with a fragile-looking blonde ash frame and brown vinyl upholstering. To his surprise it was luxuriously comfortable. To pass time he began thumbing through a back copy of *Air Progress* magazine, the May 1978 issue, with a cover photo of a Vultee BT-13 converted to look like a Japanese Val dive-bomber.

"Mr. McDade?"

The Penetrator glanced up to see four men widely spread in a semi-circle before him. Their clothes, the way they carried themselves and the blank, stern looks on their faces said, *cop.* Two of them produced guns, the third a pair of handcuffs. Their leader stepped slightly forward.

"Mr. McDade, you are under arrest. Let's do this peacefully, shall we? Please stand and submit to a search."

Mark complied, wondering at how easily he'd been taken. Since his career as the Penetrator had began, he had accepted the possibility that some day he would walk into the path of a bullet, or turn the wrong corner and get his skull crushed, or turn the key in car or airplane and be blown into tiny red bits of dead meat. That was an acceptable part of the risks he took. Somehow, though, the thought of being busted by four Alabama policemen had never entered his consciousness. For the sake of form, however, he went through all the usual motions.

"What's going on here? Why are you arresting me?"

"I really don't know, Mr. McDade. Charlie, pat him down."

Another burly cop stepped up to Mark and ran his hands lightly and expertly over his body. From the pocket of the Penetrator's sport coat he removed the High Standard .22 Magnum derringer, the only firearm Mark had brought.

"We can add a concealed weapons charge, too, Sarge." He snapped the cuffs into place on Mark's wrists.

"Hey! I got a right to know the charge against me."

The Sergeant replied in a low voice. "All I know is we got a call from the attorney general's office, said to come over here and take you into custody. When we get to the station, I'm sure you'll find out what it's all about."

They hustled the Penetrator out the door, down the elevator and across the lobby to a car waiting outside. Silence held as the crowded vehicle worked through traffic and took US 231 north out of town. Whatever their destination, the Penetrator decided, it wasn't the local jail.

Two hours and forty minutes later the car pulled into the drive between two tall stone gate posts at Pine Grove Plantation. The Penetrator had no doubt now that his "arrest" had not the least official status. That told him something interesting about Jim Bolt, too. An ironic smile twitched the corners of his mouth.

"Johnny Herter sure seems to have a lot of people on the pad."

"Keep runnin' that mouth, asshole. It's like a backhoe diggin' your grave." The so-called sergeant turned around in the front seat, glowering at their prisoner.

The driver stopped the car in the barnyard area and dumped Mark onto the dirt floor of an ante-bellum-period smokehouse. Once the door closed, a sweet-acrid odor of oak and hickory smoke permeated the air in the dimly illuminated room. Getting out of the cuffs would prove no problem at all, the Penetrator thought. Nor would escaping from the smokehouse. Leaving Pine Grove might prove a little more difficult. He went about formulating a plan while freeing himself from the manacles.

Mark slipped his fingers between his belt and trousers, prying open the Velcro closure of a long, narrow compartment built into the leather. From inside he extracted a handcuff key and unlocked the cuffs. Next he seated himself on a ledge near the door, on the blind side where he couldn't be seen when it opened. Then he undid his belt, pulling out the leaf-bladed push-dagger that formed the buckle. The Tom Enos improved version of Sandy Brygider's original concealed-knife belt had come to the Penetrator's aid often in the past and he felt confident of its beneficial contribution to his present situation. All he had to do now was wait and plan.

"Of course I know what I'm talking about, Johnny." Larry Flowers paced back and forth in Herter's plantation office, carrying the phone with him, his voice agitated with excitement as he talked to his boss. "We've got the Penetrator locked up right here in the smokehouse. . . . It was easy. Jim Bolt called, told us this guy was there with almost the whole story on Wells and a lot of other stuff. From the description he gave, Charlie and Fred Golinsky both said it was the Penetrator. Fred sent a crew over and I headed straight up here. . . . No, we didn't have time to tell you first. But we've got him now and I'll swear, by God, it's the Penetrator. What do you want done with him? . . . Okay.

We'll take good care of him until you get back here."

Mark tensed as he heard the lock and hasp rattling on the other side of the smokehouse wall. When the door swung open, the broad-shouldered shadow of a man projected onto the opposite wall. The Penetrator heard a startled gasp.

"Wha . . . where the hell is he? The thick-necked gunman surged into the room without any thought for his own safety.

The Penetrator stepped quickly behind Charlie and looped one heavily muscled arm over the man's shoulder, his hard hand closing tightly over the open mouth. Mark's right arm came up, placing the razor-edged blade of the push dagger against Charlie's throat. He spoke in a soft whisper.

"If you want to keep on living, let go of that piece."

Charlie obeyed, dropping the Smith & Wesson M76 submachine gun he carried. The Penetrator released his hold over Charlie's mouth and, before the guard could call for help, shoved him violently forward. Charlie's head collided with an ancient, heat-hardened eight-by-eight, making a solid *klunk*. He sagged on elastic limbs and fell to the dirt floor. The Penetrator crossed quickly to him and relieved the unconscious man of a .38 Detective Special which he tucked in his waistband. Then Mark retrieved Charlie's S & W M76 SMG.

The Penetrator didn't think too much of the guard's choice of firearms, but it beat the hell out of bare hands. He checked the magazine and pulled the bolt back into firing position. Then he slipped cautiously out of the smokehouse. He closed and locked the door to help delay discovery and began to stroll purposefully toward a pickup truck some fifty yards away.

"Hey, where do you think you're going?" The challenge came from a man lounging in the shade of a tall barn. "Where's Charlie? . . . Unh! It's an escape! Stop where you are! Get somebody out here, it's the Penetrator. He's tryin' to escape!" The shouts were punctuated with gunshots.

Mark raised the S & W sub-gun and silenced the shouting guard with a five-round burst. Then he sprinted to and vaulted over a low stone fence. Almost at once bullets slapped into rock, a few whining away in richochets. The Penetrator returned fire and sprinted toward safety in a line of pines that lay beyond a plowed field.

Slugs thudded into the ground to either side of the Penetrator, sending up plumes of dust and small clouds. More rounds whirred past his ears. Zigging and zagging, Mark Hardin gained ground, swinging his right arm behind him and firing blind. He didn't expect to hit anyone, only to break up the concerted drive of his opponents. As he neared his goal he made out the blurred form of another stone fence, screened by a jumble of weeds.

The Penetrator stopped long enough to face his enemy and chop off another five rounds, cutting the legs from under his two closest pursuers. Then he tackled the five-foot stone barrier. As he rolled over the top, a bullet slammed into the rock near his head with such force that it blurred his vision. Letting go, he fell to the other side. His head felt pummeled, his eyes ached, and he squinted to try to clear his vision.

Slowly his eyes regained their focus and Mark

found himself looking at a pair of worn boots, surmounted by faded Levis. Shit. He'd come this far only to be taken captive again. Above the denim trousers he took in two sun-browned hands gripping a shotgun. At least he could go out fighting. If he judged correctly, he had six or seven rounds left in the M76. Mark started to swing the SMG up onto target.

"You won't be needin' that, feller. Any enemy of Johnny Herter and his mob is a friend of mine. Especially if he's takin' shots at them. My name's Jesse Deerhorn."

All but two persons, Samantha Chase and Johnny Herter, had left the old supermarket building campaign headquarters. Following the Selma trip—of which Sam had heard few details—where the merger with the Democratic Party would be announced, the party apparatus would be moved in here, the American People's Party signs being replaced by the Democratic donkey. As a result, Sam had been given an assignment that greatly aided her real purpose. She was to winnow files, making room for the new material. It gave her an excuse, though a somewhat weak one, to dig into places the average party worker never saw. She looked up from her examination of a financial document as she heard footsteps.

"Ah, Ms. . . . ah, Chase is it?"

Samantha smiled encouragingly. "Call me Sam, Mr. Herter."

"All right, Sam." Herter moved closer, placing one large hand on Sam's shoulder, fingers straying idly to her auburn locks. "My loyal supporters call me Johnny. I hope you're one of my loyalest ones."

"Of course . . . uh, Johnny. I had two helpers on this job, but they left hours ago to fix supper for their husbands. Me? I don't care, because I've got no one to fix for. It's such a pleasure working for you, I simply forget about time."

"What are you doing with the financial records?" Johnny moved closer to Sam. She could feel the sexual aura emanating from the man, insistent, demanding, lustful. At least he was normal *that* way, she thought thankfully. Johnny's maneuverings gave her a chance to think up an answer.

"I was told to go through them and pull everything dated more than six months ago to put in boxes for storage. We'll have to have room for the things they're bringing day after tomorrow."

"Oh, I see." Johnny accepted her explanation. "What say you call it quits for now? I feel I owe you a drink and dinner for all this dedicated service."

And a trip to bed with the Great Man thrown in for good measure? Sam thought cynically. She made her eyes grow round and forced honeyed gratitude into her voice. "Why that would be wonderful, Mr. . . . ah, Johnny. Any girl working on the campaign would jump at the chance for a private dinner with you, Johnny. But," she let a tone of regret slip in, "can I take a rain check on it? I have some absolutely vital girl things to take care of after I finish here."

Rather than quench his desire, the refusal fired Johnny Herter's hunger to bed this newest member of the staff. He slid his arm completely around Sam's shoulder, drawing her to him. "I think we can arrange that. Are you coming to Selma? If not, consider yourself officially invited. We'll have dinner there. Do you take shorthand?" Herter's change of subject puzzled Sam, but she nodded in the affirmative. "Good. Then what say after today you are my personal secretary? You'll go to Selma in that capacity and I don't want you to leave my side for a single moment."

Whoo, boy, Sam thought, *shades of Congressman Wilbur.* "Why, I . . . I don't know what I've done to deserve this. I mean, I'm so new in the campaign. I'm sure there are other girls far more deserving than me."

"Let's put it like the kids do these days. It's because I dig on you, baby. Besides, it never hurt a candidate to have a pretty gal near him. You'll do just fine. I've had other . . . ah, secretaries during the campaign. Most of them even stayed with the organization. You better get on home now and do some packing. We leave early in the morning."

When Sam reached the furnished apartment she'd rented near Herter's campaign headquarters, the phone was ringing. She hurried across the small, dingy living room and answered it. The Penetrator spoke from the other end.

Sam's reply came out filled with self-satisfaction. "Hey, McDade! Herter wants to lay me. Looks like he's going to turn out to be his own weak link. I'm going to Selma with them tomorrow. He's so antsy he was all but panting in my ear like a puppydog."

"Be careful, Sam. This thing is getting more dangerous by the moment." Quickly Mark filled Sam in on his arrest and the battle at Pine Grove. "Herter's got the fix in all the way to the attorney general's office. We can't risk going to the authorities again until we know who all the players are. What did you dig out?"

"Not a lot more. But this secretary scam might get us what we're after."

"I'll be in Selma, too. It looks like the only thing is a DA mission on Herter, make him come into the open and show his fangs."

"A DA mission?"

"Yeah. Direct Action. Hit 'em hard and scatter around a few arrowheads. Look for what crawls out of the woodwork. Be careful, Sam. When the bullets start flying I don't want you in the line of fire. I'll meet with you before I get it going. With any luck, you'll have what we need or where to find it and I can save the fireworks for later."

Chapter 11
Campaign Trail

A genuine steam calliope shrilled its syncopated music into the air and large crowds clustered around the various attractions along the small midway set up at the Selma fairgrounds. With the backing of the Democratic Party, Herter's campaign had been given a new financial facelifting that let the candidate go all out in promoting his try for office. The Penetrator arrived early and began taking in the scene.

Mark didn't spot Sam until a little after one in the afternoon. The greased pig chase and watermelon-eating contests had been run, a whole barbequed steer consumed, and hundreds of gallons of soda pop, iced tea, and beer gulped down. Herter, with Sam at his side, ascended to the platform facing the grandstand. The space occupied by the bunting-decorated plank structure was normally used for tractor pulling and harness mule contests. In addition to seats for dignitaries and speakers, an area had been provided for the rock band, God's Blood. Scattered applause, which grew in volume as people hurried to find seats, greeted Johnny as he walked to the rostrum and adjusted the microphone. He raised both arms, palms out, to silence the crowd.

"Friends. Just before I left Montgomery to come

down here, I received shocking news. A gang of militant extremists shot up my little ol' farm, Pine Grove. They left one man dead and three wounded. Who would do such a terrible thing, you might well ask. Some of my advisors suggested it might be the Ku Klux Klan. That's a possibility, since the Klan is against everything I stand for. The police, naturally, are investigating and as yet we don't know who is responsible. Whatever their names might be, we do know this. They are radical Right-wing reactionaries of the worst kind. When they're caught, I wouldn't be surprised to find that they're also responsible for the murder of Andy Wells.

"What these Right-wing extremists are after is easy for anyone to understand. They're trying to force me out of the campaign, to intimidate me into quitting the race for senator. Well, I'll tell you this. They picked on the wrong boy. Johnny Herter don't scare easy. I'm going to stand up to these faceless, nameless gangsters and I'm going to defeat them and see them in jail. I'm gonna fight them and win because you wonderful folks are behind me. With that determination and your continued support there's gonna be a new senator from Alabama . . . and his name's Johnny Herter." The audience shouted approval.

"Now, there's some good news, too. Recently backers of the late Andy Wells, who was a very dear friend of mine, and certain members of the party's Central Committee came to me, asking if I would accept a draft motion to become their party's candidate for senator. The answer to their question is . . . yes!" Cheers broke out, led by Herter supporters strategically placed in the audience. One among them, the Penetrator didn't join in.

Quite a performance, Mark thought. *So now I'm a gang of Right-wing extremists, eh? Herter must be losing his grip to use that tired old smear.* The Penetrator's attention returned to the platform as Herter began speaking again.

"So now, my good friends, we are united in our battle against the reactionaries, the extremists, and the fat cats of capital." Another ovation began and the rock band struck up a loud rendition of Herter's campaign song.

When quiet returned, Johnny Herter spoke for another ten minutes, outlining his platform. He promised to work for reform of the welfare system with emphasis on bigger checks for recipients, for enlargement of the Department of Education, for normalization of relations with Cuba and a new policy for Latin America. He didn't come down on firearms as solidly as Andy Wells, but said rather vaguely that he would work hard to do something about their "uncontrolled proliferation." He also promised increased federal programs and funds for Alabama and half a dozen other grandiose ideas. When the cheering ended, Herter and his retinue left the improvised stage. The Penetrator followed them.

Herter's Selma campaign headquarters had been set up in a storefront along the route of the historic civil rights march. Herter's long black limousine parked in a loading zone outside. Johnny and two of his staff emerged, carrying overstuffed briefcases. Looping an arm around Samantha Chase's waist, Johnny led the way inside the building.

A spirit of extreme elation filled Herter's campaign office. The candidate bubbled with enthusi-

109

asm. Members of the staff slapped each other on the back and talked about how the campaign was in the bag for sure now. One of Herter's aides cynically asked if he couldn't arrange for some "Right-wing nuts" to shoot up one of the campaign centers. When it was empty, of course. Herter turned a cold eye on him. Sam took it all in, watching closely as the briefcases were unloaded, hoping to spot something of interest.

The outer door jangled open and Mike Parsons, Johnny's youngest aide, entered. A smile split his face nearly from ear to ear. Shouting congratulations to all he walked over to Johnny, making no effort to lower his voice.

"You sure got them all going your way now, Johnny. Still think you'll have to bring in Belman to make that other hit?"

Herter's face lost its animation, rearranging into hard, cold lines. His eyes flickered with suppressed fire and his lips drew back like the rictus of a corpse. An ominous silence filled the room after the aide's injudicious remark. When Herter at last spoke, his voice scratched as though from old age or great thirst.

"Ah . . . Sam. I just remember I left something important at the hotel. My small black attaché case. It's in my room. Here's the key. Would you mind getting it for me?"

"Not at all, Johnny. Sure. I'll go right away."

"Thank you, Sam." Herter remained silent until the door closed behind Samantha Chase. "You idiot! That kind of stupid, careless oral diarrhea can get us all jailed, Mike. What the hell made you say anything about Belman and a hit . . . another hit at that . . . in front of her?"

110

"I'm sorry, boss. I figured you were setting it up to lay her, so she oughtta be safe."

"Just because I'm planning on screwing a broad don't mean you can say whatever pops into your head when she's around. If anything, the opposite is true. We don't know a damn thing about her and here you go running your mouth . . . aaawh, to hell with it." Herter grabbed a phone and punched out a direct-dial long distance number.

"Jim? Let me talk to Belman . . . Art? You know who this is. Looks like you'll have another one to do." The brash young aide paled, thinking he was hearing his own death sentence. "It will have to come before the one we already discussed."

"Who?"

"A broad named Samantha Chase."

Sam met with Mark while Herter took his usual late afternoon nap. They sat in Mark's car out on County Road 37, which led to Summerfield and Valley Creek State Park. Mark listened as Sam explained about the chance comment by Mike Parsons.

"After a slip like that, it's a wonder you're still around, Sam. So they carry their confidential information around wherever they go? It makes sense. Removes the possibility of someone prowling the files while they're away. It's time to get you out of there, Sam. Too damn dangerous. We'll knock over their secret files and head for Montgomery."

"When?"

"Tonight, while that dance is going on."

"I'll have to think of something clever to get away. Herter plans that dance as a big prelude to jumping into the sack."

111

"Simplicity is the key, Sam. The more complex your excuse, the more transparent it becomes. Why not go to the little girls' room and not come back? With all the distractions Herter'll have being guest of honor, by the time he figures it out, we'll be out of his office and away from here."

God's Blood had vibrated the walls of the Civic Auditorium and deafened human ears with their blatting ya-ya music for two hours when Mark and Sam met outside the Selma campaign headquarters. The Penetrator produced a set of lock picks and they entered after only two unsuccessful tries.

"There's a safe, Stan. No doubt they locked that stuff up for the night."

"That's what I brought this gadget along for." The Penetrator produced a small electronic device on a magnetic base. It amplified the tumbler sounds of a combination lock and displayed the correct number in a digital readout.

Sam led the way, kneeling beside Mark as he examined the small vault. An old Gates. Given half an hour's time he could open this crackerbox without any aid but his bare hands. It would be a four-number combination, probably starting to the left, counterclockwise, since most people's instinct would be to begin in the opposite direction. He attached the little black box and spun the dial.

After two and a half turns, a small, red wheat-grain bulb on the face of the device flashed, indicating the first tumbler in place. Since he wouldn't be opening this safe again, he ignored the numeral displayed in softly glowing scarlet figures. Back to the right now. In only half a turn, the second pin fell. Back to the left one turn and another one out of the way. Marvelous. Someone, in a burst of originality, had no doubt set the combination to his birthdate. Now to the right again.

Nothing happened. Tricky, a double left at the end. The Penetrator cursed himself for not making a notation of the numbers. He'd have to start all over again.

"Left two and a half to twenty-one, right a half to three, left one to five," Sam whispered.

Mark quickly worked the combination to that point, then turned further to the left. A slight, audible click sounded. He turned the locking handle and swung open the safe door. "There we are. Now let's see if this was worth all the effort."

Dividing the safe's contents between them, they began going rapidly through the papers. Speed reading one page after the other, Mark extracted several dealing with future plans to rip off coal on public lands. Sam worked quietly, nibbling on her lower lip with small, even white teeth.

"McDade, look here. Here's a list of public officials, judges, law-enforcement types. I wonder how many of them Herter owns?"

"We won't know until it's checked out. Better pull it to take along."

"And here's a file on Nelson Lemmon. Hmmm." Sam set to studying each page. "Oh-oh. Look at this." She handed the Penetrator a single slip of paper, taken from a personalized note pad Herter kept beside his telephone. On it were printed words, "T date, Tues. 10th."

"That's the day of the primary."

"Could be that's the hit Belman is supposed to make that I overheard them talking about."

113

"It sounds crazy, but you might be right, Sam. What better way to insure winning an election than by eliminating all of the competition? First Wells, then Lemmon. But Herter would have to be a lunatic to seriously consider that."

"From the look on his face when that kid let slip his comment about Belman, it wouldn't take much to convince me Herter isn't playing with a full deck."

"Gather up anything else you can find of importance and let's get out of here."

Ten minutes later the files had been returned to their resting place, the safe door closed and locked. Mark and Sam started toward the front of the building, the Penetrator carrying the evidence they'd found in a black attaché case with his safe-cracking tools.

Suddenly the front door crashed open, glass tinkling as it hit the wall. Two shots blasted orange-yellow light into the room.

Chapter 12
Fugitives from Justice

The Penetrator's superb reflexes saved them both from death in that first instant. At the sound of the inward crashing door, Mark dropped the attaché case, falling away to his right as his left arm flashed out, straightarming Sam in the opposite direction. They both huddled on the floor by the time the first two shots were fired.

"We know you're in there. Come out with your hands up." Another shot punctuated the remark of the man in the doorway.

The fourth round in the brief gun battle was not heard by anyone. When he dropped to the floor, Mark Hardin drew his Colt Commander fitted with an extension barrel and sionic silencer. A wheezing, whistling, *plock!* of sound, a greatly reduced muzzle flash, and the metallic clacking of the slide gave the only evidence of the weapon's discharge. Even in the darkness, the Penetrator's aim proved true.

In the doorway, the big man with the gun jolted backward, turning slowly to the right. He took a tentative, uncoordinated step, then went slack, crumpling to the sidewalk. At once, one of the large plate glass windows dissolved into a shower of fragments under a sustained, but unheard, burst.

Someone out there with a silenced sub, the Penetrator thought, moving further to his right and forward to get a clear view of the street. From his left, Mark heard a soft whimper, quickly stifled. Sam? Surely she couldn't be getting the jitters under fire after what happened in Mozambique. The Penetrator could see the man with the submachine gun. He stood near the center of the sidewalk, slightly crouched, legs spread wide, holding the stubby Uzi SMG before him, probing the night air with the bulky suppressor affixed to its muzzle. Mark took careful aim.

The Penetrator's slug caught the man high in the chest on the right-hand side, with enough energy to dislocate his shoulder. He screamed with pain, fell to the pavement, and dropped the Uzi to clutch at his injured side. In the same instant, the Penetrator surged to his feet, making a dash for the doorway.

"Go for it, Sam!"

"I took a hit, McDade. Go on without me."

"The hell with that." Mark reversed his course, found Samantha Chase, and helped her to her feet. Together, they hurried to the door. When they came cautiously out onto the sidewalk, they met further resistance.

George Nesta, driver of the gunmen's car, watched his companions get gunned down in rapid succession with a wondering sense of disbelief. These guys were good, some of the best in the business. Yet there they lay, one dead, the other bleeding all over the sidewalk. He'd served in Nam with Ray Hollander, the dead man in the doorway. After their discharge they'd drifted from one futureless job to another until hiring on at Paragon Security. That their work often bordered on the illegal didn't

116

bother either of them. The realization that he alone remained to face the unseen marksman in the building did nothing to bolster George's self-confidence. It did even less when he saw the movement of two shadowy figures at the door.

Nesta's hand sped toward the butt of the piece he carried in a shoulder rig, as he dived across the front seat of the car, toward the open passenger door. His first shot went wild. He didn't get a chance for a second one.

Mark's first slug gouged hair and scalp in a deep trough along George Nesta's head. It knocked the man unconscious, so that he didn't feel the second bullet that slammed into the top of his left shoulder, jolting his body violently as it bored in, missing the subclavian artery but burrowing deep into flesh behind his left lung. Mark hurried to the LTD sedan and dragged the comatose, bleeding Nesta from the front seat. He motioned to Sam, who came staggering slightly, to slide into the front seat. Mark closed the door and legged to the other side, climbing behind the wheel. The engine fired effortlessly and they rolled away at a moderate speed, hoping to give possible witnesses little to remember. From near-by, growing closer each second, came the wail of sirens. Forgotten in the battle, the evidence that had cost them so much to gather lay behind them in Herter's campaign headquarters.

A clanging bell, followed by three 10kc beep tones attracted the attention of every police officer in Alabama who happened to be listening to the radio. A calm female voice followed, giving information quickly noted on clipboards in police cruisers.

"Headquarters Barracks, Alabama State Police.

Transmission One-Seven-Niner. Attention all law enforcement officers. Time: 2100 hours. A five-state all points bulletin is being issued on a fleeing subject. Warrants are pending on subject charging: first-degree felony homocide, assault with a deadly weapon, assault with intent to commit murder, kidnapping, first-degree burglary, breaking and entering, and grand theft auto. Suspect's description is as follows:

"Subject is known as the Penetrator, proper name unknown. He is a white male American, age 28–30, six feet to six-four, 205–210 pounds, black and brown, dark complexion, prominent nose and cheek bones, barrel chested, with broad shoulders, medium build. Visible scars on right jaw, sickle shape, gash on left side of neck. Subject was last seen driving a stolen 1979 Galaxy LTD, license : Alabama 23J758. Subject is armed and considered extremely dangerous. Do not attempt to apprehend without assistance. If subject is sighted, notify Colonel Ashton B. Lathrop, Commandant, Alabama State Police.

"According to information provided by witnesses, a second person is believed to be traveling with subject and presumed to be a hostage. She is Samantha Chase, white female American, age 27, five-foot-eight, red-auburn, yellow-green, no distinguishing features, marks or scars.

"Subject and his hostage fled Selma, Alabama, following a shooting incident at the political campaign headquarters of Johnathan Herter. Mr. Herter identified the Chase woman as his personal secretary. Victims of the assault were security officers of the Herter organization. Further bulletins will follow as information develops. Transmission One-Seven-Niner ends."

The Penetrator thanked whatever providence had equipped Paragon Security vehicles with police monitors. The car they occupied was hotter than the main furnace in hell. They'd have to ditch it. Mark had driven out of Selma on State Highway 219, heading north. He wanted little-traveled roads tending generally toward Gadsden and Herter's plantation. For a while Sam bled severely from a shoulder wound. She had finally managed to bandage it crudely but effectively enough to stop the blood loss. They had turned onto State 25 at Centerville and again onto S-119. They neared Oak Mountain State Park, south of Birmingham, when the broadcast automatic signal turned on the radio. When it concluded, Mark looked over at Sam, who leaned slackly against the opposite doorpost.

"We're going to have to dump the wheels. How are you feeling?"

"Sleepy. And about as strong as a new-born kitten."

"I'm sorry, Sam, but we have no choice."

"How far are we from Gadsden?"

"About a hundred and sixty miles, give or take."

The Penetrator selected a fire lane, cleared among the trees in the state park. Turning into it, he drove up a steep, winding grade. He stopped at last, drawing in under a canopy of pine boughs. Smiling through his concern for Sam, he helped her from the car.

"Looks like we hoof it from here."

"We lost the evidence, McDade."

"Don't let it worry you. The way I'm going to handle this now, we don't need evidence."

"Meaning?"

"I'm going to waste Herter."

119

* * *

"Call it off, Johnny. We can't let this . . . this torpedo hit Lemmon now. Not with everything that's happening. The heat is on good. It's beyond anything we can control." Porter Carson sputtered in his effort to make the candidate understand.

"I can't think of a better time, Porter." Back in Johnny's plush office in Montgomery, Herter, Carson, and Dave Guthrie met to discuss the situation that was breaking around them.

"I agree with Porter, Johnny. We'd be fools to go on with it now. Hell, the FBI is in on the deal, there are more cops swarming around everywhere than flies on puke. Look at it the way they'd have to.

"At the beginning the Democrats had two candidates with you on the outside. Wells gets hit. You move in as his replacement. Still two candidates, right? If Lemmon gets taken off now, who does that leave as the logical suspect? You're the only one to benefit from both killings."

"Oh? Let's look at it from *my* angle, shall we?" Johnny Herter began pacing the office floor, confidence puffing him up at each stride. "Wells is killed, right? Then Pine Grove gets shot up, after that my campaign office in Selma. My secretary is kidnapped as a hostage. At least that's the way the cops bought our version of it. In both of these shooting incidents the Penetrator left behind blue flint arrowheads, like he did in Scottsboro when he made a try for Belman. Okay, what does that buy us?

"I talked with the agent in charge of the FBI team. Goodman's his name. He flew in special from Washington. He's so anxious to pin something on the Penetrator . . . and catch him at it . . . that

120

he'll take anything we tell him as gospel. Now comes the clincher. We didn't give the cops all those arrowheads that got scattered around. Belman has a couple of them. It's all set up. So when he makes the touch on Lemmon, he leaves them behind. Now who gets blamed? That's right, the Penetrator."

"Oh, my God." Realizing that Herter's ambition and plans had gone far beyond control by any of them, Porter Carson lowered his suddenly tired head into shaking hands.

Chapter 13
A Matter of *Orenda*

High above, the sun burned hotly down from a point just past the zenith. A helicopter, its insectile body casting a huge shadow on the ground, hovered over a quadrant on the east side of Oak Mountain Park. Slowly it rotated on its axis, giving the occupants a 360° view of the forest below. Then the motor for the main rotor revved up and it slanted away through the sky, like a prehistoric winged beast seeking its prey.

"Close." The Penetrator's voice came out a thirst-roughened croak.

"And getting closer. We've only made about seven miles in ten hours. McDade, I can't make it. If we stick together we'll both be caught. Go on without me."

Mark gently raised Sam to her feet from where they'd crouched hiding from the chopper. "Don't talk crap, Sam. We'll be out of this in a couple of hours and then we can pick up another car."

"Another stolen one? The only way to get out of this is to walk out and you can only do that alone. My shoulder hurts, I'm tired . . . I'm thirsty. I'm so terribly thirsty." Mark and Sam had been without food or water for over twenty hours, since long before their visit to Herter's campaign office. The strain showed plainly on Sam's drawn features. The Penetrator tried to bouy up her sagging will.

"That's the blood loss. Another reason we have to reach help. C'mon. Let's go. One foot in front of the other."

Three hours later, their march constantly interrupted by slow, low-flying Cessna 172's and the ever-present helicopter, Mark and Sam staggered out of the last screen of pines into a grassy meadow. Wildflowers dotted the green expanse, vivid flashes of white, yellow, blue. Their throats were seared speechless with thirst. Sam swayed dizzily and Mark had to make a conscious effort to keep one foot moving in front of the other. They'd been on the move for thirteen and a half hours, unable to locate drinkable water and constantly having to hide from their hunters. As Mark urged Sam onward, two dark spots appeared in the distance, on a crescent shaped rise of ground that formed the dam for a large pond.

Calves, the Penetrator thought. Sam moaned brokenly and sagged, falling to the ground. Mark dropped to his knees beside her. When he next looked up, two small, brown-skinned boys stood near-by, panting from the exertion of their run, their black hair still wet from swimming in the pond. They were both stark naked, but showed not the least self-consciousness.

"*Sha-nta naheten shawee'na.*" A language rich in glottals, but strange to the Penetrator's ears crackled from one youngster. The other boy turned and ran off in the direction from which they'd come. The remaining kid took a step forward, eyes twinkling with excitement as he spoke in English. "Don't worry, Mister, we'll get you some help."

124

Help. That meant a cool drink of water, a chance to rest and to hide from the persistent searchers. The thoughts burst in Mark's head like ideas of the greatest import. "Okay, kid. Thanks, thanks a lot," he answered. Then the Penetrator sat down beside Sam. He closed his eyes for what seemed only a moment.

When the Penetrator opened his eyes he saw three men standing close. The newcomers looked like adult versions of the boys who'd found them. One handed Mark an earthenware jug full of cool water. The Penetrator took a little, worked it in his mouth and let it trickle down his aching throat.

"Can you talk? Are you all right?"

"Y-yes. I'm okay now. But Sam . . . she's hurt."

"Relax. We'll carry her. I have a truck down by the pasture fence. We'd better be going."

Samantha Chase regained consciousness stretched out in the back of a bouncing pickup. The first thing her eyes focused on was a sign: WELCOME TO CHICKASAW.

"W-what's Chickasaw?"

The two boys, now dressed in cut-off Levis, giggled.

"Chika-*shay*," the Penetrator corrected. "Alabama is one of the states in the Union that doesn't have an Indian reservation. But it seems like we've stumbled onto a community made up of original inhabitants."

"You sound like a college professor." Sam accepted a second small sip from the jug. "Mmmm. That tastes better than moonshine."

"That's what was in it before Dad emptied it out," the elder of the two youngsters offered.

125

"Maybe that's why it tasted so good."

"Better take it easy, Sam. No more bubbling repartee. You're a long way from being well."

"Sam? How come you call a *girl* Sam?"

Samantha turned her head until she could look at the bare bronze chest and pug-nosed face of the younger child. "My name is Samantha. Now would you like to be stuck with something like that?"

Both boys made faces that indicated extreme repugnance. Mark laughed, despite his condition. Regardless of all she'd gone through, Sam retained her sense of humor. And she seemed to have a natural rapport with kids. The truck stopped outside a large old clapboard house.

An hour later, Mark had been fed, bathed in a sun-warmed horse trough in the backyard and dressed in soft boots, smooth, well-worn Levis, and an open collar shirt. His own clothes, including his Resistweave jacket, were being laundered. Sam rested in a comfortable bed upstairs. Her wound had been cleaned and treated by the local doctor, who was also a Chickasaw. Mark made a rapid recovery and was soon able to down an entire glass of iced tea without feeling nauseated. He set down the sweat-beaded tumbler of his second drink as his host entered the room.

"It's time to go. They're ready to see you now."

Mark didn't bother to ask whom it was wanting to see him. What troubled him, as they climbed into the pickup, was what the outcome would be of his meeting with what must pass locally as a tribal council. Both men remained silent during the short drive to the city office building.

A large gathering crowded the mayor's office.

126

The mayor was there, of course, along with the chief of police and two uniformed officers. Also present were the doctor who had treated Sam, the city attorney, an ancient, wrinkled, gray-haired man, and Mark's host, who had introduced himself as Herbie Shotuma. Mark took the chair indicated to him and sat, head up, facing his examiners.

"There's no reason to waste everyone's time with some long-winded tale, young man. We know who you are. . . ." At a glance from the mayor, the chief, and his two men drew their revolvers. "It is the decision of the majority on this council that you be turned over to the state police."

"Do I have the right to say something before you haul me away?" At the mayor's nod, the Penetrator continued, though now he addressed them in the ancient medicine language common to many tribes of North America, Mexico, Central and South America. He spoke for three minutes, telling of his need to be able to continue, explaining Herter's criminal acts and the reason the security guard had died. Then he said a few words about himself, why he knew this strange, secret language.

When he concluded, there came grunts of amazement from around the room, words of agreement and dissent. Mark crossed his arms over his chest and tilted up his chin, waiting stoically for the results. To his momentary surprise, it was the doctor who answered him. But then, Mark thought, what more logical profession for a medicine man to take in the white man's world?

"You speak as a Brother of the White Buffalo Lodge. A such, we must listen. Some still do not believe. You mentioned a Red Eagle. We know of one Red Eagle. He is said to be a wanderer, an ancient

127

shaman of the Beautiful People who travels from one tribal band to another, bringing the ancient ways and past glory of the People to their youth. It is also said he gives young people a new pride in their heritage and a desire to make a better life than that on the reservation. These things are good."

The Penetrator listened to the musical flow of the doctor's words in the medicine language. He waited the proper number of seconds at the conclusion of the speech to politely show he paused respectfully to see if anything more would be said. Then he nodded gravely.

"It was my humble honor to be his ignorant student."

"*Hau! Hau!*" The word of approval rose from the lips of the ancient seated near a tall, narrow window. "You speak with the proper respect for one's elders. Would that some of these puppies would show the same consideration to their gray-heads."

"Old Grandfather, you know better," the doctor said, using the respectful term reserved for older persons. He had a pained expression on his face. "So now what do we do with you?"

From the corner of his eye, Mark noted that the service revolvers had been returned to their holsters. He remained silent, letting the doctor work it out for himself.

"What is it you need?" You can, of course, hide here as long as necessary."

The conversation had reverted to English and Mark pressed his point eagerly. "We . . . at least I have to go on. Herter must be stopped before the primary. There is a man, Jesse Deerhorn. Do any of you know him?"

"He is one of this council," the mayor informed Mark.

"If I can get to his farm I still have a chance to expose Herter. Can you let me use a car or truck?"

Chad Crowfoot, the chief of police, stepped forward, shaking his head. "That's not so good an idea. You could be spotted. There's roadblocks, that sort of thing. Yet there is one way."

"Right, Chad." Herbie Shotuma left his chair, came to stand beside Mark. "Herter's throwing a big party tomorrow. A junior rodeo, pow-wow, all that. At Pine Grove. No doubt he wants to cover all bases and get the Indian vote, too. What I'm getting at, the whole town's emptying out for it. There'll be a caravan of trucks, horse trailers, and the like. Some are leaving tonight, others in the morning, take your pick. They won't search us that close and it will be easy for you to hide."

"Perfect. We'll do it that way. Now, will you be able to look out for Sam until this is over?"

"Sam's in good shape and she's going along." Samantha Chase stood in the open door, a sputtering secretary trying to wedge herself between the determined young woman and the meeting in the mayor's office. "Don't give me a hard time, McDade. The deal was we worked this together."

"Unless it got too dangerous. And a bullethole in the shoulder is too damn dangerous in my book."

"Stuff it, McDade. I'm going."

About three the next morning, the caravan made a brief stop outside the entrance to Jessie Deerhorn's farm. Two figures, keeping to the shadows as much as possible, detached from the convoy and started up the dirt farm lane. As soon as they cleared the edge of the road, the trucks and cars moved on. Jesse Deerhorn expected his late-night visitors and let them quietly into the darkened house.

"Ah, the man from the fence line. You are the subject of a great deal of notoriety, my friend. Who is the lovely young Miss with you?"

Mark made the introductions. "Jesse, you told me you believed someone should knock Herter right out of the saddle. Things have happened, never mind what, that make that the only alternative. To do it, I'm going to need some ordnance. Can you get your hands on any explosives? Any firearms, automatic weapons in particular?"

"Explosives I've got, of sorts. On gettin' any guns, I'm afraid the choice is limited. Me 'n Steve have shotguns, and he's got a .375 Wetherby, though I don't know what the hell he intends to shoot on this continent."

"How about that old wheel-gun, Dad?"

"That's right. It's an old single-action Colt. My grandad left it to my father and I let Steve butcher it up for fast-draw shooting."

"Is that an original 1871 SA?"

"Right, black powder forty-five Long Colt. But I've got a couple of boxes of ammo for it."

"Okay, Jesse. We'll have to settle for that if necessary. Between us we've only got twenty-four rounds of forty-five ACP. What about these explosives?"

Jesse grinned at the Penetrator. "You're really gonna do it up brown, aren't you? Well, I got about a half case of dynamite and a bunch of fuse caps. Then there's the fireworks I was savin' for July Fourth. Three- and five-inch bore skyrockets and

130

aerial bombs, some big fat stick rockets, some of those screaming things that run along the ground. That sort of thing."

"Hmmm. Might serve as a diversion. Okay, so here's the plan. We're going to use this big gathering as a background. What we have to do is show that Herter isn't what he's supposed to be. . . ."

A little before dawn the next morning, Harmon Catchesraven managed by persistence to get through security and talk with Johnny Herter personally. They met in Herter's office at the plantation house. What he had to say caught the candidate's attention immediately.

"That's all of it, Johnny. You know I've always liked you and appreciate what you've done for me and the AIM chapter I'm trying to get going. I was there on the chief's orders. We were all set to bust him, then he starts talkin' in the old language and suddenly everything is buddy-buddy. I ain't learned that stuff yet, so I don't know what they said. Anyway, they dropped them off at Jesse Deerhorn's, right next to your place."

"I appreciate this, Harm. Really I do. We'll handle it from here on in. There's a thousand dollars in it for you. That's the reward I offered for information on this guy. Soon's we've had a chance to check it out, the money is yours."

"Thank you, Johnny. Thanks a lot. Any time I can do anything for you, just holler. AIM's gonna back you in the election, don't you worry."

High ridges to the east kept direct sunlight out of the valley for some time after sunrise. Jesse Deerhorn's farmhouse sat in a pool of Stygian night when headlights suddenly swept across the front and side, mixed with blood red and blue flashing lights. Three cars roared to a noisy stop, their beams focused on the clapboard dwelling. After a moment's pause, a voice grated through a bullhorn.

"This is the sheriff's department. We don't want any trouble. Jesse Deerhorn? Are you in there?"

"Oh, damn, we're raided." Jesse crossed the living room to the front door, peering out through the beveled glass oval set in its center, before opening up. "I'm here, Jed. What do you want?"

"We've got word that a dangerous fugitive is in the area, might be seeking more hostages. You alone?"

"Is that Jed Barns?" Sam asked. At Jesse's nod, she went on. "Then we're in deep trouble. He was on Herter's list of bought officials."

Chapter 14
Empty-Handed

"And *that* takes care of that!" A great peal of laughter accompanied Johnny Herter out of his office. He entered the breakfast room of the plantation house where his guests waited. Accepting a cup of coffee, poured by a servant, he took his place at the table.

"Gentlemen, our fortunes have taken another upturn. I just heard on my police monitor that at this very moment the Penetrator," he let cynical humor creep into his voice, "scourge of all evil-doers, is being apprehended by local sheriff's deputies. Our troubles from that source are over."

"I certainly hope so. I can't help but think that he was after us on the coal deal."

"Relax, Albert. You and Mort here have nothing more to worry over."

"I'm not so sure," Morton Sutter, querulous by nature, had a rasping, buzzing voice. "We've made millions out of this coal from public lands. Sixty-five million the government claimed a couple of years ago, but it's more like one hundred and fifteen. Now that we've opened this new strip mine behind Pine Grove, it's no time to be matching wits with someone as dangerous as the Penetrator. Oh, I know, once you're elected to the Senate, we will

133

have ample protection. But you aren't elected as yet."

"After tomorrow there'll be literally nothing to stop me. As the only candidate for the party, I'll be a cinch to win. The state's always gone Democratic, so it doesn't matter who the Republicans put against me in November. With the Penetrator being taken out of our way by the law, we ought to be celebrating. Now, let's get to business. You have how many new sites to open? Six is it? How do we cut the pie?"

Literally no way existed to pass off Sam's presence in the Deerhorn house. Jesse gave it quick thought and made a suggestion.

"The outdoor oven. It connects into the kitchen through the wall. Crawl all the way in there. Then, Steve, you lay a fire, only don't light it. Now, what do we do about you?"

"I'll worry about that while you hold off the law."

Mark Hardin started through the house, taking a narrow stairway to the second floor. In the closet of one bedroom he located a trapdoor leading to the attic. He stood on tiptoe to nudge aside the square panel, then gave a slight jump. Mark executed a pull-up to draw his long frame inside. He slid the cover into place and stood as high as the sloping roof would allow. He'd have to set about finding a place to conceal himself among the clutter.

The Penetrator moved cautiously. A fine patina of dust covered everything. Rearranging a few items to cover the minimal marks of his passage, he slid into position behind a large, dome-topped wooden steamer trunk and drew his silenced Colt Commander. From below he could hear Jesse's muffled voice, raised in protest.

"You got a warrant, Jed?"

"Don't be stupid, Jess. We don't need a warrant. This follows under the rule of hot pursuit. We got a tip this Penetrator desperado was around here, maybe holdin' you an' Steve hostage, so we're gonna come in even if it ain't covered. You sure you're all alone? No one in another room holdin' a gun on you?"

"We're all that's here."

"Okay, Steve. I believe you, but under the circumstances, you understand we have to search anyway." Jed Barnes turned to the other deputies who had streamed into the house. "Two of you stay here, the rest go outside. Search the barn, the chicken house, that old shed, and the outhouse. Don't leave anything out, ya hear?"

The search began, moving from room to room on the ground floor. Jed Barnes twice looked into the combination cookstove and outdoor oven, opening the cast-iron door and peering in at a large teepee-shaped pile of thin sticks and shavings. At last he asked why the fire wasn't burning.

"Just getting ready to fix coffee when you came storming in here."

"Coffee sounds good. Why not put it on?"

"Ah . . . I will. Soon's we get done upstairs, Jed. That's only kindling and I don't want to get shot by some nervous deputy while going outside for wood."

"Yeah. Some of them boys ain't too bright."

Upstairs proved as unrewarding as the search of the lower floor. Jed Barnes ordered it done over again. This time one deputy found the attic entrance. The lid was thrown aside and one uniformed man climbed up, moving with enough vigor to raise clouds of dust. He sneezed violently.

"Nothin' up here, Jed. Just a bunch of old junk and . . . and . . . " Another sneeze erupted explosively. "Dang dust."

"Look around, damnit! We know he's here somewhere."

"Sure, Jed." Another sneeze. "Hand me up a flash."

Five minutes' hurried inspection completed the deputy's effort. He moved about, his actions punctuated by almost constant sneezing, checking behind and over piles of discarded items. Once the Penetrator swung stealthily up onto a rafter, hanging silently there while inches below him the young sheriff's man shined his flash into the space Mark had previously occupied, sneezed, and turned away. Eyes streaming water, the officer returned to the attic door and let himself down.

Downstairs again, Jed turned to the Deerhorns. "Now how about that coffee?"

Steve hesitated. Then at a glance from his father, he walked into the kitchen and applied a match to the kindling. He shut the door and started to pour cistern water into a granite coffee pot.

"Awh, never mind that, Steve. We ain't got time for it anyway. I just wanted to see you light that fire."

As soon as the police cars started up and turned into the lane, Steve dashed to the kitchen and threw the pot of water into the stove. A choking, red-eyed Sam crawled out onto the floor. Her clothing showed ample soot smudges and smelled of wood smoke.

"My Lord, I thought I was candidate for the main course at breakfast." Sam rose unsteadily to her feet.

"More likely it would have taken till suppertime to get a good do on you." Jesse busied himself making coffee in an electric percolator. The Penetrator joined them and Jesse turned back from his task, a wide grin on his face.

"Well, score Round One for the Redskins."

"What the hell do you mean they weren't there?" Johnny Herter rose from his swivel chair so abruptly it upset, crashing to the floor. "I swear, Jed, those deputies of yours are so stupid they need retraining every morning to tie their shoes."

"We searched every part of that place. I even made Steve Deerhorn start a fire he had laid in that old ovenstove thing. The guy could have been hiding in there, but I wasn't about to poke my head in and get it blown off."

"Okay, okay. So you did as well as you could. What about the girl?" Johnny seemed deflated by Jed's negative head shake. "Crap. Now get out of here and set up road blocks all around the place. They're around here somewhere, so help me." Once Jed Barnes had departed, Johnny turned to Dave Guthrie.

"Dave, you round up some of the boys. Fill them in on what's going on and then send them to Deerhorn's place to do the job right."

137

Chapter 15
Pyrotechnic Picnic

"I'm all right, I tell you. Don't even bother to say it, I'm going in on this operation." Sam and the Penetrator were in Jesse Deerhorn's barn, working to convert their limited explosives supply into something useful. "All that rare meat and . . . *yitch*! . . . half-raw liver Jesse's been stuffing down me makes me feel like I could bite nails and spit out thumbtacks."

"It doesn't matter how good you *feel*, Sam. What counts is what kind of shape you're in. You lost a lot of blood. You were half-dehydrated and bounced all around the countryside in a drafty horse trailer, then nearly turned into a smoked ham. Considering your physical condition, you have to see that taking you along would only be a liability."

"Liability, my butt! Anyway, I don't intend to assault the bastions like the Marines at Chapultepec. I've worked out a little plan that should make your job easier."

"Pass me another stick of that dynamite."

"You're not listening to me."

"Yes I am. You said something about the Marine Corps, right?"

"McDade! You're a rat. Look. I think I can get away with sneaking in that place like any of a

139

hundred jiggle girls Herter will have for his special friends after the pow-wow is over."

"Hey, you're wanted, too. As far as Herter is concerned, that is. He wants you alive, no doubt for his own little plan of revenge. Wouldn't do to have you alive and talking, no matter what happened to me. How do you expect to go unnoticed in that place?"

"All I have to do is cut off these old Levis, just short of showing everything I have. I'll figure out something for the top-side. A little dye job on my hair and some loud make-up and there won't be a male eye in the crowd on my face. I can carry enough dynamite in my purse to create a dandy little diversion. That should give you a boost. Well, wouldn't it?"

"Sam, Sam, Sam." The Penetrator sighed heavily. "I'll think about it. That's all I can promise right now. We have to finish here and get this in place before ten-thirty or so tonight. Once that's done, we'll see."

"I'm gonna do it. You know it and I know it. I'm gonna do it."

They continued working in silence. Sam poked holes in the sides of sticks of 60 percent nitro dynamite, inserted fuse caps with two second fuses crimped in place. These she handed to Mark, who taped them to the long wooden sticks of large commercial skyrockets. He then made a small slit halfway up the fat tube of propellent charge and inserted the open end of the fuse, taping it securely. The added weight of the explosive would, Mark knew, reduce the altitude and range of the rockets. But he hoped that the result would provide for the dynamite going off close to the ground at the end of their short flights. Their task took them another hour. At

140

the end of that, they began converting other fireworks.

Sunset's ruddy glow still lingered in the west when Herter's men finally worked themselves into position near the Deerhorn farm buildings. Herter had sent Lenny Young, his top man, along as leader. Young gathered his men together in the shelter of a clump of hickory trees near the barn.

"Okay, you guys know what to look for. This dude's supposed to be a big one, broad shoulders, Indian lookin'. You see him, you start blazing away."

"What if it ain't him? What if it's one of the guys who lives here?"

"So what? We're gonna waste them all, eliminate witnesses. But try not to burn the girl. The boss wants her brought back alive. Now, Rudy, you and Craig go around to the other side of the barn, keep an eye on the back door of the house. Ivan, you go down there where you can cover the front. Dix, you watch the side and front of the barn. I'll take the house from here. Okay, move out."

Five minutes later Lenny felt sure his men were in place. Darkness cut a sharp line between the valley floor and the ridge to the east. Light suddenly spilled into the farmyard from an opened door.

On the opposite side of the yard from where Lenny crouched, Rudy Garcia and Craig Aishman brought rifles to their shoulders and began squeezing the triggers as a figure appeared in the door.

Steve Deerhorn's combat-honed reflexes warned him of danger the moment he entered the bright frame of the door. He pushed the tray of sandwiches and coffee away from him and dived off the back

141

steps while twin muzzle flashes turned the night yellow-orange.

Inside the barn, the Penetrator jumped to his feet when he heard the first two shots. Another round blasted off as he grabbed up Jesse Deerhorn's shotgun and headed toward the back entrance of the barn.

"Didn't think Herter would give up this easy. Stay put, I'll be back."

Carrying the twelve-gauge Winchester loosely in his left hand, crouching low, the Penetrator left the barn, circling out and to one end. He reached the edge and started along a low corral fence. He had already drawn his silenced Colt Commander and as he neared the corner post, he snicked off the safety and peered around.

A short distance away he spotted Dix crouching in a position to cover the front entrance of the barn. Mark brought up the Commander and squeezed off a round.

The Penetrator's bullet struck Dix in the right shoulder, smashing the ball-and-socket joint and creating such intense pain that Dix's mind blanked out in self defense. He gave an involuntary moan and toppled, unconscious, to the ground. Mark reversed his course and headed toward the opposite side of the barn, from where the shooting continued.

Ka-blam! Jesse Deerhorn's round from the big .375 Wetherby Magnum kept Rudy's head down. Craig blasted off again, his slug striking the window frame near where the elder Deerhorn crouched to return fire.

"Ya all right, Steve?"

"Yeah, Dad. Creased me along the shoulder's all.

Throw me that Mag. I'm better with it than you are."

Jesse cut loose with another shot and tossed the rifle out the window to his son below. He then went into the kitchen and returned with his son's shotgun. Double-ought buckshot sprayed the leaves among the lilac bushes where Craig and Rudy had concealed themselves. They quickly decided it was time to find a better position. They rose and started off, to step into the Penetrator's slashing fire.

A shotgun with 00 buckshot is a deadly combination at close range. Unfortunately, Mark hadn't been close enough. Two pellets dug into the fatty tissue under the skin of Rudy Garcia's right side. He screamed in pain and stumbled off into the darkness. Craig Aishman, who had turned his head to one side to check their line of retreat, caught one pellet through both cheeks, which broke some teeth and brought on a flood of crimson that drowned out his cry of pain. He also took a lead ball in the meaty portion of his left thigh, a third and fourth smashing the stock of his rifle. He dropped the useless weapon and stumbled off toward the front of the house.

Still uncertain of how many enemies he faced, the Penetrator moved cautiously, covering the same ground that Craig had taken. As he reached the corner of the front porch, he saw movement in the near distance. Two figures, one clutching his wounded mouth, ran in the direction of a line of trees. Mark peppered the ground around their feet with buckshot to hurry them along. He started for the far side of the building.

While the Penetrator ran he shoved two rounds into the tubular magazine. Jesse's shotgun had been plugged for hunting, limiting the capacity to three rounds. He came to the end of the porch and zigged around it to the corner of the house. Taking a deep breath he popped his head around for a quick look. Mark jerked back when he saw the wink of a muzzle flash. Extending the barrel of the shotgun, he pumped the old '97 Winchester rapidly, holding down the trigger, so that he sprayed the twenty-seven pellets from the three rounds into the foliage near where the ambusher had shot.

Lenny had a choice to make as the pellets slashed leaves and splintered fence rails around him. He could stay and carry on the firefight or he could get the hell out of there. It took no great ammount of intelligence—something Lenny lacked enormously—to figure out which constituted the better idea. He quickly joined the other three in retreat. As his feet pounded into the distance, the Penetrator broke cover.

When Mark passed near the barn, Sam called out to him. "What shall I do with this one? He's bleeding badly."

"Hold him. We'll question him later."

"Not much later from the looks of it." Her words barely reached the Penetrator as he caught sight of the fleeing men. He let go another blast from the shotgun, rewarded this time by a yelp of pain. Ivan stumbled and fell, two pellets in his buttocks. Dix slowed long enough to help his comrade to his feet and they stumbled on. The Penetrator fished into a jacket pocket for more ammunition and found he had expended all but the two in his weapon. His fingers did brush the comforting presence of the plow-handle grips of the .45 Peacemaker. It rode on his hip, stuffed inside his belt. Then he found himself on the receiving end of incoming rounds.

Recovering somewhat from their initial rout, the quartet of gunmen stopped their flight to burn off a few shots in the direction of their pursuer. Panting, Lenny briefed his men.

"We gotta make it back, let the boss know what's happening."

"I'm gettin' weak, Lenny. This hole in my mouth is bleedin' again." Craig spat blood and swayed with fatigue and weakness.

"Hang on, Craig. You come with me, the rest of you split up. He can't get us all."

A thin scudding of clouds obscured the waxing moon that already hovered over the mid-sky point. It made the Penetrator's task more difficult. He came to the place where the gunmen had split up, noting the irregular trail left by one of them. The Penetrator had already reached the same conclusion Lenny had concerning the importance of the would-be ambushers reaching the plantation. That was something Mark couldn't allow to happen.

It could result in the fight being brought to him, placing him at a considerable tactical disadvantage. Armed as they were and headed toward where help could be obtained, he saw no way to stop them short of killing all four. The idea didn't appeal. Wasting men in a firefight Mark accepted as part of the game. Methodically tracking them down, one by one, and exterminating them he didn't exactly appreciate. Given a him-or-them basis, though, he had to accept the necessity of it. Reconciled to it, he continued studying the ground.

One of those who had split off ran with shorter steps, indicating fatigue or a serious wound. Mark moved out after this one, steeling himself to the task of killing all four.

The Penetrator came upon Ivan quickly. The gunman staggered slightly, favoring his right ham where the 00 buck pellets lay in his flesh. He turned at the sound of Mark's footsteps, trying to bring up his rifle. A single round of 260-grain round-nose lead punched into his belly, smashed a vertebra to splinters, and severed his spinal cord. It ended his resistance along with his life. To save time, the Penetrator broke into a fast lope, cutting across the diverging paths. Knowing their destination he needn't return and start a new trail.

He missed making contact with Lenny and Craig, but a study of the ground showed him that they were greatly slowed down, merely walking instead of running in ground-devouring strides. He pushed on. Swinging constantly to his right, he neared the general area where he expected to find the last man. Eyes to the trail, he went doggedly on. In so doing he nearly walked into a fatal ambush.

Three shots burnt holes in the night. The bullets zipped and moaned into the darkness, close enough that one of them cut through Mark's trouser leg, searing a painful gouge across his left calf. He stumbled, turned it into a fall, and lay motionless, the hammer already racked back on the old single-action Colt. His super-sensitive ears quested for the slightest sound.

Rudy moved. The brittle, summer-browned pasture grass crackled under foot. He stepped again, taking the most direct route to the man he felt he'd finished off. A wide grin creased his face as he identified the darker form against the blackness of the ground. He raised his pistol for an insurance shot.

Then the one thing happened that could totally ruin his day.

The Penetrator's finger twitched against the feather-light, fast-draw altered trigger. The big spur hammer fell and the air filled with the dull thump detonation of black powder. It bloomed also with a cottony sphere of smoke that obscured the Penetrator's vision.

Rudy reared backward as the big slug caught him high in the chest. He almost lost balance, to fall head first, but managed to right himself and start forward again. Then he realized that somehow he must have dropped his gun. He bent to look for it.

At the same instant, the Penetrator decided to end it quickly. He brought up the Winchester and let off one of his remaining two rounds. All nine pellets entered flesh, splashing large quantities of Rudy's upper torso, neck, and face into the grass for several feet around. The Penetrator came to his feet and started off after the remaining two.

After climbing over the low stone fence, Craig passed out. Thinking they were safe now, Lenny lifted the lightweight man in his arms and staggered on. He started off making good time. Being the only unwounded man he had an advantage. Lenny sighed with relief when the moon came out from behind the clouds, better lighting his unsure path across the field. He remained confidently unaware that death trailed him by a matter of seconds.

The Penetrator reached the wall dividing Jesse Deerhorn's land from Herter's. He didn't want to risk breaching any electronic alarm system Herter might have, but he had to stop the other two men. Over the wall he went. Then the moon came out and he saw in the distance the lurching form of

147

Lenny. The other man's legs dangled over the gunman's arms. It was too far a shot to risk on the shotgun. Mark leaned it against the wall and drew the Peacemaker.

He racked back the hammer and took aim, settling the fat-bladed front sight in the notch, then raising it until he centered its base in the rear aperture. Gently he squeezed off a round. A slight breeze cooperated by blowing away the billowing cloud of smoke. He'd missed, but not by much. The target had broken into an awkward, shuffling run. One more try.

This time he had no need of a clear field of vision. He heard Lenny's cry before he stepped aside and saw the man sagging to the ground. The Penetrator loped to where Lenny had fallen and checked both men. Craig still lived. A quick bullet in the side of his head ended that. Then the Penetrator began a hasty withdrawal.

Back at the barn he got little out of Dix, the fifth gunman. What he did learn was beneficial. The team was not supposed to report back to Herter. They wouldn't be missed, likely, until too late. Before Mark could ask more, Dix died.

"I did get a good layout of the plantation house," Sam informed the Penetrator.

"Good. I'll need it."

"*You'll* need it?"

"That's what I said. Let's get that stuff set up. We haven't much time. How's Steve?"

"No sweat. A little crease that Jesse washed and bandaged. He'll be sore and a little stiff for a few days, no big thing."

"All right. Let's get to the fireworks."

148

Chapter 16
Compound Felony

"Before concluding, my dear friends, let me say this. My opponent in the primary election will be the incumbent, Nelson Lemmon. He is a man of strong conservative opinion, who has the courage of his convictions. Too bad he was born a Democrat. Because during his six years in office, it seems as though Mr. Lemmon's priorities have been at odds with the needs of the people he was elected to represent. That's why I say we need a fresh new face on the floor of the Senate.

"Though the primary is the real battleground, we can't afford to let our guard down once it's over. We need to be gearing up for a fight now, with an eye toward the November election. Thank you." Johnny Herter quit pacing about his office reciting lines of the speech he would deliver at the Indian dance contest that concluded the festivities at his plantation. He turned to where Art Belman slouched in a large leather chair.

"Well, how's that?"

"Why waste all that air on Lemmon? When I get done tomorrow he won't be a candidate."

"I'm supposed to act as though I already know it? Maybe refer to him as the *late* Nelson Lemmon? C'mon, Art, you've got better sense than that."

"Oh, I get ya. If you're on record psychin' your troops up to fight him, you can't possibly be a suspect when he gets wasted. Good idea."

"Now you're tracking, Art." Johnny would have said more, but a quick knock interrupted him. One of his aides entered the room.

"Mr. Fields and Mr. Sutter are here again, sir. They have some gentlemen from up North with them."

"Okay. I suppose I have to see them. Art, take a walk, huh? Go enjoy yourself. The real party will be startin' once we get rid of these Heap Big Injuns."

Art Belman left the office and a few minutes later Herter's aide ushered in Albert Fields and Morton Sutter. With them came two men with bushy Ivy League hairstyles and boyishly smiling mouths that duplicated the fashion of the dynamic young senator they worked for. They looked hot and uncomfortable in the tightly fitting three-piece suits, formal white shirts, and subdued ties they wore. Their harsh, nasal, Harvard accents grated on the ears of the others in the room, accustomed as they were to softer Southern vowels. Johnny Herter forced a welcoming glow.

"Al, Mort, good to see you again." Introductions were made and chairs filled.

"Let's get right to business, Mr. Herter," Bryan O'Banyon began. "These gentlemen have been in conference with our principal, and others who are favorably inclined, for the past several days. We feel that a cooperative agreement can be struck. The bottom line is this: How much are you taking and what would be offered to other senators giving their patronage?"

* * *

Drums throbbed in heartbeat rhythm and the high-pitched voices of old men wailed the words as brightly costumed warriors stomped, whirled, and gestured their way through the intricate steps of a scalp dance. A line of women advanced and retreated in repeated steps, each advance taking them nearer to the circling braves than they lost in backward steps. Each woman and girl held aloft a willow branch frame from which dangled tufts of black Dynel hair, symbolizing the war trophies celebrated by this ancient ritual. Pine Grove Plantation's small rodeo arena was brightly illuminated by huge, flickering bonfires. The dancers continued, unaware of the work being completed less than five hundred yards away.

Mark, Sam, and Jesse Deerhorn finished their installations while the drums maintained their beat. Mark gave instructions to Jesse as to when he and Steven were to start setting off the improvised mortar rounds. Then they headed back to Jesse's house.

"You know, I get the feeling the two of you ought to be over there dancing with the rest."

"That's a scalp dance," Jesse told her.

"My point exactly."

"Why's that, Sam?"

"This whole operation is like something right out of *The Last of the Mohicans*, McDade. While the French enemy and their allies dance their victory, trusty old Squantum leads the Redcoats into position for their dawn attack."

"It wasn't Squantum, he was chief of the bad Indians. It was . . . was . . . oh, hell, I've got a mental block."

"It was Uncas," Jesse said quietly.

"Right. Anyway," Mark continued, "I'm not making a dawn attack."

"You mean *we're* not."

"We've been over this subject to the point of exhaustion, Sam. You are not going and that is final."

"You gonna tie me up to stop me? Or shoot me? Look, I've got the shorts ready, little cuffs rolled up to show lots of thigh and Steve's lent me a see-through tank top that, worn braless, will guarantee no eye will be on my face. I can handle myself, I have my gun, and I'll have enough dynamite to scare the bejesus out of anyone who might, and I said *might* recognize me. I'm going."

The Penetrator surrendered to the inevitable. "Okay. You'll have to leave about half an hour before me. But be it on your own head. I still don't think you should go. Move in when the crowd breaks up after the dances. If you can work it, drift along with those invited to the after-party at the big house. But stay away from Herter and his people."

"I have it down already. Good luck . . . and be careful."

"You're the one that needs to take special care . . . and have all the luck."

Sam dressed hurriedly and left Jesse's place as the crowd began to break up around the small arena. She received many admiring looks, and a few disapproving glances from the distaff guests, as she worked her way toward the main house. Ignoring Mark's admonition to stay clear of the area of greatest danger, she cut through the poolside patio, entered the building, and began to place explosive charges in out-of-the-way places. She chose a kitchen cupboard, a ledge inside a large fireplace—

unlighted on this warm summer evening—and put smoke bombs in hallway niches, under upholstery-skirted furniture, and in shadowy corners of the tile patio around the pool. She also scattered a handful of whistling chasers, each with a six-minute time fuse made of two pipe cleaners saturated in a solution of saltpeter and dried in an oven. Twisted together end to end and tightly coiled they well served the purpose. Her work done in the house and immediate area, Sam began placing her nasty little distractors in strategic spots around the outside.

Everything so far had gone according to her plan. Few of the late-night revelers had as yet arrived and she had most of the place to her herself. She worked her way along the bedroom wing of the mansion and found she'd run out of materials. Well, she'd withdraw and wait for the attack to begin. Sam rounded the corner and ran face-to-face into Art Belman.

The Penetrator watched the second hand of his watch cross the hack mark and vaulted the low stone fence separating Jesse Deerhorn's farm from Herter's plantation. He sprinted the first few hundred yards, passing the undiscovered corpses of Lenny and Craig and learned why he hadn't tripped any alarms earlier. Herter's first electronic security screen was installed a good fifty yards beyond where Mark had finished off the two gunman.

The Penetrator cleared the invisible beam with a running jump and came up against a roving patrol of men and guard dogs.

Chapter 17
A Drop in Popularity

Fangs bared in silent snarls, the dogs leaped forward, slipping their lead chains as one of their handlers fell wounded and the other reacted quickly, though not so fast as the Penetrator.

Mark had his silenced Colt Commander in his fist from the moment he was committed to the attack. He brought it up at sight of the patrol and shot one man in the hip as he reached for the walkie-talkie hanging from his belt. Mark's second round took the lead dog. The open, slavering mouth of the Doberman swallowed the slug that blew out the back of its skull. A well-placed, toe-first, front kick deflected the other pooch from its course. The animal whimpered pitifully as it struck the ground, broken rib ends puncturing its lungs. The Penetrator pivoted toward the second guard.

Seeking to conserve ammunition, Mark advanced on the man, taking the *Eagle Claw* attack stance of *Orenda Keowa*. The man drew a revolver, whipping it out so fast that it veered far off target. At the same time he placed a whistle in his mouth, inhaling deeply to give it a long blow. Regretting the expenditure of another shell and the necessary death of the guard, the Penetrator shot him in the chest, trying for perfect bullet placement.

155

Mark's aim didn't prove as true as he hoped. The hollow point slug cut a crescent out of the left side of the man's sternum, punched through the aorta, and snapped a rib clear of its juncture with the spinal column. Blood gushed into the guard's chest cavity and his whistle drowned in a spew of blood. Making sure of his kill, the Penetrator walked to where the injured dog lay. Moisture filled his eyes as he looked down.

"Sorry, old fellow. It isn't your fault." He didn't regret the use of *that* round. He took time to smash the small radios and club the other guard unconscious, then he hurried on. Behind him, Mark heard the dull report of mortar tubes as Steve and Jesse Deerhorn ignited the first of the fireworks.

Suddenly the sky filled with a plethora of bright colors. A gigantic globe of golden lace expanded like a mini-galaxy, showering down over the Herter plantation. Reds, blues, and greens followed, soft pops of their detonation coming behind the bursting sky lights. As a second battery began unfolding, the Penetrator moved out, heading for the plantation house.

Most of Johnny Herter's special guests had congregated around the swimming pool. They acquired drinks and began to munch from the exotic delicacies displayed on a long buffet table. Their attention, like that of most of the guards, went skyward as the fireworks began to burst. A voice called out in the crowd.

"You gotta hand it to Johnny. He sure comes up with some great ideas." Others made agreement, some applause scattered through the milling group, and laughter rippled along with appreciative *oohs* and *ahhs*. Suddenly their enjoyment turned to uncontrollable terror.

A fat-bodied skyrocket bounced off the roof and fell into the pool area, going off just above the bamboo-faced portable bar. Beautiful blue-and-white fire-flowers blossomed from it a fraction of a second before the stick of dynamite attached to its stick-fin detonated. The blast flattened the moveable saloon, seriously injuring the bartender, who lay unconscious in the rubble. Women screamed and fell in a heap as the blast hit them. Dust obscured the patio and the dazed crowd began seeking any means to escape. Then Sam's hidden bombs began going off.

A large chunk of wall bulged out, then took off in graceful flight to land in the swimming pool. A tidal wave splashed over the sides, swamping panicked guests off their feet. The sliding doors to the living room strained a moment in their frames and disintegrated into flying fragments of glass shrapnel. Whistling chasers screamed down hallways to explode at random. Suddenly the scene dissolved into World War III in bright, awful colors and frightening wraparound sound. Bedlam descended as more blasts fell out of the night, trailing thin orange lines of sparks.

Even Art Belman was momentarily distracted by the fireworks, staring with hypnotic awe for two slow dragging seconds at the display above him. He had been dragging Sam along, away from the house, toward a distant barn. He'd recognized her from the photo provided by Herter and he didn't intend to be done out of his hit money by turning her over to the candidate, no matter what the orders. When his forward motion arrested and he gazed at the sky, Sam decided to make her move to escape.

She aimed at Belman's head, swinging her purse, heavy with the two-pound weight of her stubby Detonics .45. At the first flicker of motion, Belman came back to his surroundings and ducked. He lashed out with a hard hand, smacking Sam on one ear. It staggered her but she tried to renew her attack, using a reverse-hand sword stroke toward Belman's exposed diaphragm.

The hired assassin blocked her first blow easily, stepped in, deflecting her second lunge, and delivered a palm-heel strike to the nerve center under Sam's jawline. Flashes of white, green, and black blinded her and Sam sagged at the knees, head lolling as she slipped into light unconsciousness. Belman scooped her up in his arms and continued along his route.

Dodging from tree to tree, seeking to avoid the path of the terrified guests, fleeing the earth-jarring explosions behind them, the Penetrator advanced on the plantation house. He broke into the clear and noticed another man, carrying the limp form of a woman, heading toward him. As he watched, the dangling female seemed to revive and begin struggling violently against the man's restraint. Closer now, Mark recognized Samantha Chase. Mark leaped forward.

In the same instant, Belman recognized the Penetrator. He dropped Sam, clawed out his pistol. He snapped off the safety and spent a fraction of a second in indecision, debating whether to finish Sam off first or get the man who had been lousing things up from the beginning. He decided to answer first the threat of the Penetrator's gun. At his feet, Sam struggled to open her purse. Belman swung his Browning onto target and loosed a round that whistled uncomfortably close past Mark's ear.

The Penetrator went into a combat crouch, both hands on his .45, squeezing gently. Belman's second bullet smacked into a tree inches from Mark's face, stinging him with sharp, high speed slivers. Then the Penetrator ticked off his shot.

Two .45's blasted together, both slugs entering Belman's head. Sam's came from below, catching Belman under the chin, making a ragged hole in his tongue on its way to his brain. Mark's 185-grain death-bringer plowed into the narrow space between Belman's eyes and put out his lights forever. Shaken, Sam came to her feet with the Penetrator's assistance.

"Shall we take the objective together?" In the distance, strings of firecrackers went off, sounding like an infantry regiment in the assault. Most of the security men rushed in that direction. "I must say, your timing is incredible." Sam brushed dust from her cheek, checked her shoes to discover a broken heel, kicked them off to go on barefooted. She gave Mark a timid grin.

"Okay, Sam. Let's go get 'em."

Shrieking party girls, some half-clothed, some entirely nude, raced past them in unseeing terror, seeking to escape the devastation that rained down on the plantation house. A short sprint brought Sam and the Penetrator to a side entrance. A *whooshing* blast of a stick of dynamite going off in the swimming pool put out the few remaining lights in the patio area. Two short rounds fell in the farmyard, flattening the smokehouse where the Penetrator had

159

been confined a few days ago. Sudden silence seemed to stun them as much as the fusilade.

"That should be the last of it. Let's go."

Inside, Sam tugged at the Penetrator's sleeve with one hand, pointing the direction with the Detonics .45 in her right fist. "The office is this way, if we want to look at Herter's records."

"That's the name of the game, Sam. But watch it, we don't know if everyone is out as yet."

They proceeded along the hallway, checking rooms as they came to them. They found only frightened, sobbing people, huddled together as if for mutual protection. At the end of the corridor a thin slice of light showed under the door to Herter's office. Mark motioned Sam to one side of the frame while he took the other.

The Penetrator leaned out and blasted two shots into the lock case, then kicked in the door, springing back out of the opening.

A scything line of slugs screamed through the doorway, burying themselves harmlessly in the wall across the hallway.

When the jury-rigged barrage began, the two Yankee political aides dived for protection behind Herter's desk. Bleating with terror they looked frantically around them with glazed eyes. "My Lord, what are those explosions? Whose using those . . . those *guns* out there?"

"Relax, O'Banyon, you're going to be using one yourself if you want to get out of this." Johnny Herter smiled sardonically. So the battle was being brought to him. Okay in his book. When all this damned noise got over, it would still come down to one-on-one. Johnny felt confident he could win any such contest. "Either of you ever hear of the Penetrator?"

O'Banyon paled with fright. "Jesus Christ! He tore hell out of Boston one time. I was there. You should have seen it. You mean . . . *he's* . . . out *there*?"

"Him and maybe a couple of others. When they get in here, though, we'll kick his ass."

"Not if he's anything like he was in Boston. Took on a whole Mafia family, torn them a new asshole. He wound up burning their best stronghouse down around their ears. Is there any other way out of here?"

"If we need it. Hang tight, O'Banyon. Here's a rod. With that big gun collection your boss has, you ought to know something about them. Dave, you an' Larry here check your pieces. You, too, Seager. We'd better make ready for them."

No one inside the room heard the Penetrator's silenced Commander. They did see the antique cast metal lock case shatter into fragments and the door fly inward. Dave Guthrie and Larry Flowers fired at the same time Johnny Herter did, sending a second fusilade on the heels of the first. They waited as only silence followed.

Then a short, fat cylinder with a greasy-looking, reddish-brown wrapping arced into the room. A trail of orange sparks sputtered from a half-inch piece of black fuse.

"Down! Dynamite!" Herter added action to his words.

The dynamite exploded with a vicious crack, deafening every ear in the room. The air filled with smoke and plaster dust and the splitting-headache-making fumes of burnt nitro. Coughing brokenly,

Johnny Herter retreated to the bookcase behind his desk. He decided the time had come to get his VIP guests out of there. Fighting down another spasm, he called to them.

"You want out of here O'Banyon, Feeney, get over here!" As the shadowy forms crawled across the floor of the darkened room, Herter hollered at Dave Guthrie. "You three hold them, Dave. Can't let these guys be caught here."

Herter swung a lower section of the bookcase away, revealing the back side of a low spirea privet hedge and the clean night air outside. "Get movin'." He shoved O'Banyon through the opening with a harsh command.

Using the smoke, dust, and confusion as a screen, the Penetrator charged into the room while Sam, crouched in the doorway, covered him. Mark saw movement toward one wall and fired instinctively. Randy Seager yelped in pain, dropped his gun, and fell to the floor, curling into a protective foetal ball. Return gunfire came from two spots. Dave Guthrie crouched behind Herter's desk, Larry Flowers knelt, exposed near the center of the room. The Penetrator turned toward the offered target, the fat muzzle of the sionic silencer lining up at eye level.

"Don't shoot, man. I give up." Flowers threw his revolver toward a far corner and raised his hands. The Penetrator made a curt gesture that included Sam. She nodded her understanding and shifted her aim to cover the prisoner. The few seconds by-play gave Dave Guthrie the break he hoped for.

He sprang up and fired a shot at nearly point-blank range. The slug hit the Penetrator in the chest under his left arm. Under normal conditions it would have been a fatal wound. But the super-strong synthetic fibers of Mark's Resistweave jacket and shirt partially robbed the bullet of its force. Originally designed as a substitute for steel belting in radial tires, the closely woven, incredibly tough strands absorbed the energy so that the 9mm jacketed round barely broke Mark's skin. Only a slight trickle of blood oozed from the point of impact. It would make an enormous bruise, though. The kinetic force of being shot staggered Mark, and as he stumbled in an attempt to regain his balance and bring his gun to bear, Dave Guthrie dodged out of sight.

When Guthrie disappeared behind the desk, Sam's bullet smacked into the wall behind where he'd been standing. Being pulled off her primary mission of guarding the prisoner gave Flowers an opportunity to bolt for freedom. He scuttled across the room and out the open escape hatch built into Herter's floor-to-ceiling wall of books. The Penetrator found momentary cover behind an overturned couch. From his jacket pocket he took a fat, red-paper-covered, four-inch-long "Cannon Cracker." Although not as powerful as a half-stick of dynamite, the big firecracker would suit his present purpose. Wincing at the ache growing in his left armpit, he lit the fuse and tossed it behind the desk where Guthrie hid.

When the firecracker went off, Guthrie reacted in the manner the Penetrator had predicted. He shot up from behind the protective wooden bulk shouting in fear. He came into view in time to take two slugs in the chest from the Penetrator's Colt Commander. The Browning High Power dropped from Guthrie's lifeless fingers, breaking the glass on Herter's desk top. Guthrie crumpled then, smearing the cracked surface with blood.

"Hurry, we don't have much time." Mark gestured Sam into the room and they began pulling out drawers and checking contents of attaché cases, looking for hard evidence to present against Johnny Herter.

From outside came another series of explosions as Jesse and Steve fired their final salvo. Over the uproar and yells of frightened people the wail of police sirens could be heard in the distance.

Chapter 18
Political Grind

"What about Herter?" Sam's question came suddenly, while the Penetrator worked to open the wall safe.

"Let him go for now. We can track him down easy enough. What we need is solid, substantial evidence to turn over to those lawmen types you hear rushing toward us."

For the first time, Sam took conscious note of the sirens. "You're right. Let's get busy."

Outside some minor fires still burned, yet no one made any effort to put them out. There were few people left on the grounds of Pine Grove Plantation to pay atttention to such problems. The swimming pool was filled with debris and was slowly draining through a crack caused by an underwater explosion. Johnny Herter's empire, along with his dreams of power, had melted away under a shower of starshells. Herter, himself, frantically sought escape.

When Johnny joined his visitors from up North on the other side of the hidden exit to his office, he found situations greatly changed over the amiable agreement earlier in the evening. O'Banyon and Feeney headed directly toward their Cadillac, one of only three cars remaining in the parking area.

"We've got to get out of here. After all that's happened it would prove extremely embarrassing to be found here when the police arrive."

"Sure thing, O'Banyon. This is only a temporary setback. We can recoup down at Montgomery."

Patrick Feeney stared at Johnny Herter with contemptuous disbelief. "Are you kidding? This has the stamp of a Penetrator job, all right. No matter what his methods, there's one thing everyone knows about the guy. Anyone he goes after, it's a safe bet that person's involved in something crooked. We're not going to be dragged into a deal like that."

For a moment, Johnny Herter stood speechless. The two Yankee politicos climbed into their car. "Look, we're in this thing together. You can't just dump on me. Take me along, will you?"

Herter's appeal was lost on Bryan O'Banyon. "Fat chance. Get this through your concrete skull. We're not involved if we aren't here when the cops come. Our principal is seeking a nomination, too, remember? There's a lot more at stake in that than your two-bit coal rip-off. He can't afford to be associated with losers . . . especially those on their way to jail."

"O'Banyon, Feeney, for God's sake, you've got to help me!"

Bryan O'Banyon started the smooth-running engine and activated the electric window. "You lost the ballgame, Herter. Get the fuck out of the park."

A cloud of dust and gravel boiled from under the rear tires. O'Banyon spun the wheel counterclockwise until the nose of the Caddy swung out of the parking lot and lined up on the blacktopped drive. With a tire-smoking screech, the northern wheeler-dealers—typical of their kind—raced away toward the safety of the distant highway. Johnny Herter stood alone in the center of the lane, shoulders sagging.

"Look at this, McDade." Sam waved a small black account book she had taken from the safe after the Penetrator had blown it open with the last of their dynamite. "The entries are in code, but the dates are in the clear. From the time period covered, I'll lay odds this is a record of who got what out of the coal stolen from public lands."

"Good. That's the kind of thing that will count. See what more you can dig out. I'm going after Herter."

"I'm coming along."

"Not this time, Sam. Listen to me. You have high credibility with the police, with other authorities. Your past with NASA insures that. How long would they listen to me? They'd be too busy wrapping me in enough manacles and chains to sink a balsawood barge to pay any attention to what I said."

"Dan Griggs could help."

"He can't and he won't. You're the only one who can put this across. Think up some good story about how and why you were here and discovered the evidence, bat your eyes at the law, and they'll buy it. They'll have to in the end, anyway."

Reluctantly, hesitantly, Sam relented. "Okay. We'll do it your way. Where do we meet afterward?"

"We don't. I said before I'm a loner, Sam. I mean that."

Samantha's eyes clouded with tears. "Oh . . . McDade. We make such a great team. We work well together and we're compatible in . . . other ways as well. Can't we meet under calmer circumstances, when there's less strain, and talk it out?"

"No, Sam. It isn't fair to you. I may be a total SOB for saying this, but there really is no other way. I've had others . . . close to me. They died messy, horrible deaths for it. I won't, as long as I have anything to say about it, let that happen to you. Now get busy, gal. Those sirens are coming closer. Bye."

"Bye for now," Samantha amended, but the Penetrator didn't hear her.

Johnny Herter ran without direction. His expensively booted feet crunched on the pea gravel of the farmyard, taking him further from the scene of his ruin. Where could he go? What could he do? Slowly a plan, born of desperation, began to form.

Al and Mort had been there earlier. More of their endless talk about the coal mining operation. They had the new strip mine going over the ridge. He could go there. They'd have to help. The whole coal scheme was theirs. They'd even come up with the idea of setting Wells up as a candidate, then snuffing him. They had more to lose than he did.

They could take him to Porter Carson in Atlanta. He'd gain some time . . . and some ground. If he couldn't have Nelson Lemmon hit, the man would be easy to beat in the general election. Even if he had to fall back on the American People's Party ticket. This whole Penetrator thing could be turned to an advantage, show the reactionary elements were after him as well as Andy Wells. People would turn out to vote for him like they never would for Lemmon. Yeah . . . it could work. It *had* to work. Altering his course, Johnny Herter started toward the top of the ridge behind Pine Grove.

* * *

The Penetrator spotted Herter as he came around
to the rear of the plantation house. Herter climbed a
white-painted rail fence that separated a large pasture from the outbuildings. He began running uphill
as the Penetrator started after him. The range was
too great for a pistol shot and Mark had only three
rounds left. He'd have to run Herter down on foot,
and the fleeing man's excellent physical condition
insured turning it into a contest. Mark let himself
relax into a ground-covering lope.

On they both ran until Herter reached a line of
pines at the upper edge of the pasture. He stopped
there, looking back. In the middle of the grassy field
he had left behind, Johnny saw the broad-
shouldered form of a man jogging along after him.
It had to be the Penetrator. Johnny drew his pistol
and took careful aim.

Herter's bullet churned up a divot in front and to
the left of Mark's course. Too far for him to risk
returning fire with so little ammunition, Mark continued to pump his legs up and down. Herter threw
another shot, the slug *whizzing* past audibly close.
This time the Penetrator stopped, gulped in a deep
breath, and held part of it to steady his aim. He let
off a single round.

Fragments of bark sprayed from a pine tree six
inches from Herter's heaving chest. Startled, Johnny
fired reflexively before he turned and began to run
again. Behind him, the Penetrator renewed his pursuit, forcing himself to greater speed.

Slowly, the distance between them began to close.
Herter disappeared among some large boulders near
the top of the ridge. A second later a slug howled
off a rock face near Mark's head, followed by the

crack of the shot. Instantly, the Penetrator changed direction, angling off between slender-trunked pines. Quickly two more shots came as the Penetrator exposed himself only briefly as a flicker of motion between the trees. Herter was running himself out of ammunition. Before leaving the protecting screen of his surroundings, the Penetrator stopped, supressing the heaving of his oxygen-starved lungs, taking the time to study the fugitive's hiding place. A pair of minutes slid silently past. Neither man exposed himself. Then the Penetrator sensed, rather than saw, movement.

Unable to bear the waiting longer, Herter made his bid to escape. An uncanny sixth-sense ability brought the Penetrator's eyes to focus on the right spot. As Herter's head and shoulders appeared between the boulders, Mark took aim and fired.

Rock chips sprayed out from a small puff of dust as the bullet screamed off into the distance. Herter cried out and clasped a hand to his neck where blood flowed freely. One round left. The Penetrator decided to save it. Using Herter's pain and distraction to his advantage, the Penetrator ran toward the man he had determined to stop.

Up over the crest of the ridge the Penetrator charged, intent on bringing an end to the chase. He floundered awkwardly in ankle-deep shale, turned into a hazardously loose slope by repeated blasting. He swayed, nearly falling, as he tried to stop his forward momentum, coming up to face Johnny Herter, who leaned casually against an up-turned pine stump. A smile of triumph widened on Herter's face. He fired his pistol. In the same instant, the Penetrator expended his last round.

Mark's bullet struck the pine bole between Herter's legs. Johnny Herter's slug cracked a large flake of shale only an inch beyond the Penetrator's body, burying itself in the stone rubble. The slides on both pistols locked in the rearward position. Stalemate.

Beyond Johnny Herter's shoulder the Penetrator's eyes took in the raw, ugly scars of a strip mining operation. Immediately below them a huge ore crusher rumbled in a haze of rock dust. Its monstrous auger ceaselessly fed the hungry maw with the contents of a line of dump trucks. Huge arc lights illuminated the Dantesque scene.

Their frozen instant ended in a savage, animal snarl from Johnny Herter. He dropped his empty pistol and seized a pine knob. Viciously swinging the weather-hardened length of root, he charged the Penetrator.

Mark shifted his feet, making ready to meet the attack. Suddenly his precarious purchase on solid ground gave way as the slithery shale lurched under him. He fell to his knees as Herter slowed to a wobbly stop over him, the deadly club beginning to descend. Even then the Penetrator was not entirely helpless.

Despite the vast distance, in time as well as space, that separated the creators of karate and *Orenda Keowa*, the two martial arts shared many similarities. Principal among these was the concept that any situation could be seized to the practitioner's advantage. As the pine knob flashed toward his exposed head, the Penetrator brought up both arms in an X block. He broke Herter's intended blow at the wrist. Sliding his left hand around into position, he applied pressure with his thumb to the little knuckle of Herter's right fist. He used Herter's forward momentum to fold and bend the man's hand back into the

171

Aikido "chicken wing." Herter lost his footing and cried out in pain as pressure built on his wrist. At the same time, the Penetrator drew back his free right arm and pistoned it forward in a vicious "spear hand" thrust under Herter's vulnerable diaphragm. The furious action, condensed into a fraction of a second, threw Herter away from his intended victim.

Although seriously injured, Johnny Herter came quickly to his feet. He clutched a jagged-edged piece of shale. Surging awkwardly through the slowly moving, slippery rock, he advanced on the Penetrator. As they closed, Herter swung his arm in an attempt to strike any part of the Penetrator's body.

This time Mark stepped inside the arc of the deadly stone and stopped Herter with a stunning forward hammer blow between the eyes. Mark's lefthanded *Shuto* chop broke Johnny's right collar bone, causing him to drop the shale flake. Using both hands to grasp Herter's wrist, Mark hurled the man away from him with an *Osotogari* hip throw. Herter landed heavily and didn't get up. The still-shifting fragments of shale continued their downward motion toward the edge, clattering musically over those below, their speed increased by the addition of Johnny Herter's mass. When Mark realized what was happening, he floundered forward, trying to retrieve the stunned man.

As Mark struggled to reach him, Johnny Herter raised himself on one elbow. Groggy and unaware of his danger, he called out to the Penetrator.

"Hey, man, let me go. I'll pay you anything you ask. Name your price. There's enough in this thing for everyone."

"No sale, sucker. I'm going to truss you up and

172

leave you here for the cops. The only paying you'll be doing is for Andy Wells' murder, among other things."

"Who gives a shit about Wells? I'm talking millions! Get me up out of here and let me walk away and I'll make you rich. I'll . . . *yaaiiiii!*" Herter's sales pitch broke off in a horrified scream as his feet and legs pitched out over the abyss. To both sides, rivers of shale cascaded over the precipice, trailing small plumes of dust. Frantically Herter lashed out, seeking to arrest his fall. His right hand grasp a small shrub near the edge, closing about its slender presence with a death grip. His motion slowed. Through fear-glazed eyes he saw the Penetrator coming closer, reaching out to grab him. Miniature avalanches of stone and dust erupted from the soles of the Penetrator's boots. It was going to work! Hope flared, rescue only inches away.

Then Herter's full weight came onto his extended right arm. The broken ends of his clavicle ground together and he bellowed in pain. Involuntarily his right hand spasmed open and he plunged over the edge. Herter's shriek of terror carried to Mark over the sound of the equipment operating below. Then it suddenly cut off.

The Penetrator dug in both heels, clawing with each hand to stop his downward plunge. He stopped barely short of following Herter off the edge. As the boiling dust cleared, he leaned over, seeking sight of Johnny Herter.

Herter lay in the trough of the auger, being slowly rolled toward the gnashing teeth of the huge machine that crushed the coal and separated it from rock. With each revolution of the giant screw, he grew nearer and nearer. No one seemed to notice.

173

The Penetrator yelled as loudly as possible, waving his one free arm and pointing to the auger. Not a single hardhat-wearing miner paid the least attention. Only a moment before entering the voracious maw, Herter regained consciousness and realized where he lay. His mouth opened in a soundless howl of pure terror, then he disappeared into the bowels of the machine.

The Penetrator felt a sour sickness rising in him. He turned away, remembering the terrible sight of frail arms and legs struggling helpless against unbending steel. With careful effort he picked his way up the treacherous slope. Weak and shaken by his battle and the struggle to survive, he at last made it to the top.

From this vantage Mark had a better perspective on things. He thought over Herter's corrupt and violent ambitions, the persons he'd hurt, the millions of dollars he'd ripped off from the American people. The Penetrator shrugged and turned toward Jesse Deerhorn's farm. His last thoughts lingered on the manner in which Johnny Herter had died.

"Well, that's what they always say," the Penetrator said aloud. "Those who aren't suited for it can sure get chewed up in the political grind."

Epilogue

There is one certain means by which I can be sure never to see my country's ruin —I will die in the last ditch.

—William of Orange

When the Penetrator returned to the Stronghold, he spent four days undergoing the purification ritual to purge himself of the blood-guilt for the lives he had taken. At the end of that time he emerged from Red Eagle's sweat lodge and dived deeply into the black pool. For the next week he spent an hour a day swimming there after his ten-mile conditioning run. By then he felt whole enough to make a check on the Situations Board.

The Operations Room of the Stronghold greatly resembled its military counterpart in any army in the world. There the Penetrator maintained his Situations Board that listed any number of sensitive developments that might turn into problems needing his attention. Factors as widely varied as the annual increase of teacher strikes and the Soviet and Red Chinese manufacture and distribution of arms in the Western Hemisphere shared space side by side. Each item received a priority number, 1–10, based upon immediacy and severity.

As it had been prior to the assassination of Andy Wells, no "Priority One" or "Two" tags appeared on the board. The Penetrator felt gratitude for that, as he examined the display. He removed the Andy Wells card, thinking of the problems the killing had caused the press and government. Neither liberals nor conservatives would any longer buy the "One Lone Nut" theory of political assassinations. They both knew conspiracies existed. But the social engineering and psychology advisors to the government still tried to sell the public on the, to them, comforting but discredited theory.

After Samantha Chase exposed the evidence linking the murders of Wells and Ed Merril to the coal scandal, clearly outlining Herter's involvement, continued insistence on a self-motivated, lone killer had a hollow, mocking sound. Oh, well, that was someone else's problem to deal with. After a single grumbling comment from Howard Goodman that he believed Mark was involved in Herter's conspiracy, mention of the Penetrator disappeared from the media. The gentle twinkling of a music box brought Mark's thoughts back to the present, reminding him of the time.

The musical notes of the overture to *Falstaff* had to come from the gold base of the crystal decanter in which Professor Willard Haskins kept his George Dickel, Private Stock, twenty-year-old bourbon. The cocktail hour must be at hand. Having had no liquor for the past three weeks, Mark Hardin discovered that he really *wanted* a drink. Contemplating his choice of potables, the Penetrator left the Situations Room to join the aged professor in the "tower."

"What smells so good?"

"Red Eagle's fixing buffalo hump."

"No fair! I just left the Situations Room and

176

there's nothing critical on the board. What's the purpose?"

"Relax, my boy. Merely a small feast to welcome you back to polite society."

"And to show appreciation of your good sense in leaving the girl behind." Red Eagle glided silently into the room.

"Sam? What are you talking about, David?" The Penetrator had a cold, gut feeling that the old mystic knew exactly what he was talking about.

"She makes a most compatible assistant, Mark. But you were wise not to draw her closer to your activities. After all, a good Dog Soldier always remained celibate when going on the warpath. The time for women came during the cold moons of winter. That's why most children were born between August and November.

"As to your own situation, it is even more important that you be most diligent in shunning the company of women. Being out of their presence and influence keeps a warrior pure for battle. There's no way of telling when you might have to pick up the pipe of war."

Mark sighed heavily. "Too true. Far too true." But at least not for a while, the Penetrator thought. Not for a while.

The Number 1 hit man loose in the Mafia jungle . . .
nothing and nobody can stop him from wiping out the
Mob!

the EXECUTIONER
by Don Pendleton

The Executioner *is without question the best-selling action/
adventure series being published today. American readers
have bought more than twenty million copies of the more
than thirty volumes published to date. Readers in England,
France, Germany, Japan, and a dozen other countries have
also become fans of Don Pendleton's peerless hero. Mack
Bolan's relentless one-man war against the Mafia, and Pendleton's unique way of mixing authenticity, the psychology of
the mission, and a bloody good story, crosses all language bar-
riers and social levels. Law enforcement officers, business ex-
ecutives, college students, housewives, anyone searching for a
fast-moving adventure tale, all love Bolan. It isn't just the real-
ism and violence, it certainly isn't blatant sex; it is our guess
that there is a "mystique"—if you will—that captures these
readers, an indefinable something that builds an identification
with the hero and a loyalty to the author. It must be good, it
must be better than the others to have lasted since 1969, when
War Against the Mafia, the first Executioner volume, was
published as the very first book to be printed by a newly born
company called Pinnacle Books. More than just lasting, however—as erstwhile competitors, imitators, and ripoffs died or
disappeared—The Executioner has continued to grow into an
international publishing phenomenon. The following are some
insights into the author and his hero . . . but do dare to read
any one of* The Executioner *stories, for, more than anything
else, Mack Bolan himself will convince you of his pertinence
and popularity.*

The familiar Don Pendleton byline on millions of copies of Mack Bolan's hard-hitting adventures isn't a pen name for a team of writers or some ghostly hack. Pendleton's for real ... and then some.

He had written about thirty books before he wrote the first book in *The Executioner* series. That was the start of what has now become America's hottest action series since the heyday of James Bond. With thirty-four volumes complete published in the series and four more on the drawing board, Don has little time for writing anything but *Executioner* books, answering fan mail, and autographing royalty checks.

Don completes each book in about six weeks. At the same time, he is gathering and directing the research for his next books. In addition to being a helluva storyteller, and military tactics expert, Don can just as easily speak or write about metaphysics and man's relationship to the universe.

A much-decorated veteran of World War II, Don saw action in the North Atlantic U-boat wars, the invasion of North Africa, and the assaults on Iwo Jima and Okinawa. He later led a team of naval scouts who landed in Tokyo preparatory to the Japanese surrender. As if that weren't enough, he went back for more in Korea, too!

Before turning to full-time duty at the typewriter, Don held positions as a railroad telegrapher, air traffic controller, aeronautical systems engineer, and even had a hand in the early ICBM and Moonshot programs.

He's the father of six and now makes his home in a small town in Indiana. He does his writing amidst a unique collection of weapons, photos, and books.

Most days it's just Don, his typewriter, and his dog (a German Shepherd/St. Bernard who hates strangers) sharing long hours with Mack Bolan and his relentless battle against the Mafia.

Despite little notice by literary critics, the Executioner has quietly taken his position as one of the better known, best understood, and most provocative heroes of contemporary literature—primarily through word-of-mouth advertising on the part of pleased readers.

According to Pendleton, "His saga has become identified in the minds of millions of readers as evidence (or, at least, as hope) that life is something more than some silly progression of charades through which we all drift, willy-nilly—but is a meaningful and exhilarating adventure that we all share, and to which every man and woman, regardless of situation, may contribute some meaningful dimension. Bolan is therefore considerably more than 'a light read' or momentary diversion. To the millions who expectantly 'watch' him through adventure after adventure, he has become a symbol of the revolt of institutionalized man. He is a guy *doing something*—responding to the call of his own conscience—making his presence felt in a positive sense—realizing the full potential of his own vast humanity and excellence. We are all Mack Bolan, male and female, young and old, black and white and all the shades between; down in our secret heart of hearts, where we really live, we dig the guy because *we are* the guy!

The extensive research into locale and Mafia operations that make *The Executioner* novels so lifelike and believable is always completed before the actual writing begins.

"I absorb everything I can about a particular locality, and the story sort of flows out of that. Once it starts flowing, the research phase, which may be from a couple of days to a couple of weeks, is over. I don't force the flow. Once it starts, it's all I can do to hang on."

How much of the Bolan philosophy is Don Pendleton's?

"His philosophy *is* my own," the writer insists. "Mack Bolan's struggle is a personification of the struggle of collective mankind from the dawn of time. More than that, even Bolan is a statement of the life principle—*all* life. His killing, and the motives and methods involved, is actually a consecration of the life principle. He is proclaiming, in effect, that life is meaningful, that the world is important, that it does matter what happens here, that universal goals are being shaped on this cosmic cinder called earth. That's a heroic idea. Bolan is championing the idea. That's what a hero is. Can you imagine a guy like Bolan standing calmly on the sidelines, watching without interest while a young woman is mugged and raped? The guy cares. He is reacting to a destructive principle inherent in the human situation; he's fighting it. The whole world is Bolan's family. He cares about it, and he feels that what happens to it is tremendously important. The goons have rushed in waving guns, intent on raping, looting, pillaging, destroying. And he is blowing their damned heads off, period, end of philosophy. I believe that most of *The Executioner* fans recognize and understand this rationale."

With every title in the series constantly in print and no end in sight, it seems obvious that the rapport between Don Pendleton and his legion of readers is better than ever and that the author, like his hero, has no intention of slowing down or of compromising the artistic or philosophical code of integrity that has seen him through so much.

"I don't go along with the arty, snobbish ideas about literature," he says. "I believe that the mark of good writing can be measured realistically only in terms of public response. Hemingway wrote Hemingway because he was Hemingway. Well, Pendleton writes Pendleton. I don't know any other way."

Right on, Don. Stay hard, guy. And keep those *Executioners* coming!

* * *

[Editors note: for a fascinating and incisive look into *The Executioner* and Don Pendleton, read Pinnacle's *The Executioner's War Book,* available wherever paperbacks are sold.]